# VANISH

Brendan Mathia

Vanish

Copyright © 2018 by Brendan Mathia

ISBN  978-0-692-97971-6

First Edition

Uncle Bill, this one is for you

# Table of Contents

# PROLOGUE

July 7, 1997, a day that will forever haunt the city of Hot Springs, Arkansas. Sidney Dobell, a seventeen-year-old girl at the time, went missing while skipping rocks with her friend, Jamie, at a branch of the Ouachita River. Jamie reported Sidney missing, but after months of searching, Sidney was nowhere to be found. The disappearance of Sidney Dobell went worldwide as this attracted many tourists.

The next disappearance took place on December 12, 1997. For this I take to a personal level. The person that went missing on that December night happened to be my father that I'll never get to meet. At the time I was still in my mother's womb, waiting to be delivered to this world that is surrounded by darkness. My father claimed that Sidney's disappearance was a hoax. His claims are the reason he is no longer here today, watching me grow up into a mature young adult. Again, my father was never found after months of authorities searching.

The disappearances became more frequent over the next few years. Finally, the FBI put up an electric fence blocking off this branch of the Ouachita River. In the summer of 2009, a group of seven men and women, filmed a documentary called, "Beyond the Fence." All seven of them made it out without a scratch, which many thought was impossible. The documentary later aired, with the cameras capturing nothing but the river and trees. Not to long after the documentary aired, they were on multiple talk shows. In their last talk show, they disclosed what was shown, isn't what's happening. They told the world to stay away and if you go, you will not make it out. The reason they made it out was because they were paid three-quarters of a million dollars. Just a few days after their confession, they were gone like they never existed. Many speculated that they oversaw whatever was beyond the fence.

On July 7, 2009 the disappearances suddenly stopped occurring. Once the FBI could confirm it was a safe area, they took down the fence, making it open to the public. I would visit the haunted branch of the river frequently, knowing that it's where my father went missing. I would sit on the river bank wondering if it was the end of the mystery.

This question would later be answered in the summer of 2015, when the disappearances began to occur again. With this, the fences went back up and the branch of the river would become a bigger mystery than mysteries like the Bermuda Triangle. With no logical explanation, hundreds of people have vanished out of thin air. This branch of the river is better known as, Sido.

# CHAPTER ONE

It's the last day of school and only a half day. On the last day of school, the administrators hold a lecture in the auditorium. The purpose of the lecture is to inform us how dangerous it is to visit Sido. The lecture takes up the whole half day. At the end students can share their theories on Sido to enlighten the mood. I've never given my theory because it isn't as interesting as everyone else's. A lot of students shared that they believe there is a zombie apocalypse occurring within the perimeters of Sido. For myself, I don't believe in zombies and if they ever do exist it's because the government created them. My theory on Sido is that there are trained assassins hiding within Sido and they capture the people to hold them as prisoners, but I haven't figured out why. I sit there thinking about if we will ever know what truly is going on in Sido.

  After the three-hour lecture, I go to lunch, then I get to go home for the summer. The saddest thing about the summer is an average of twelve high school kids sneak into Sido to never see the city lights again. At lunch, I sit with a group of friends. They talk about visiting Sido over the summer because they want to know how everyone disappears without a trace.

"Hey Dominic, do you want to go figure out what happened to your daddy?" Bryan asks laughing.

"Please don't bring my dad up like that ever again or we're going to have problems and no I don't want to go!" I say with anger.

Bryan is eighteen but still a junior because he started late, then got held back his freshman year. Bryan and I are more mutual friends than friends because we've had our problems in the past. He is the quarterback of our high school football team and is popular with his tall muscular build, sandy blonde hair, and light blue eyes.

"Oh, we're going to have problems? Let's go then Dom, I'll make you disappear like your daddy," says Bryan laughing.

I decide to do the right thing and just walk away before I snap on him. It's the last day of school and I don't need to start off my senior year suspended. When I'm walking away I feel someone touch my shoulder. Immediately, I think it's Bryan, so my first instinct is to turn around and push him. When I do this, I realize it's Bryan's sister, who I have a crush on. My eyes get big as I go down to try to save her from falling but I couldn't. When she lands she hits her head hard on the ground. I immediately drop to my knees to help her. When I do this, I see Bryan charging at me. As he is about

5

to hit me I stand up and flip him over my back. He gets back up with an urge to rip my head off.

"I'm going to kill you, you are going to cry for your daddy after I'm done with you!" says Bryan furiously.

When he goes to throw his punch, a teacher, Mr. Lokkins pulls him back and Bryan swings at the air.

"Dominic. Bryan. To the office now," says Mr. Lokkins.

While I walk to the office all I can think about is how Alyssa is doing. The whole walk to the office I shed a couple tears knowing I hurt someone I care so much about.

Mr. Lokkins tells us to sit in the chairs outside of Dr. Hawkins office, which is our principal. Mr. Lokkins opens the door to let Dr. Hawkins know that there is a problem then he closes the door. After about five minutes, Dr. Hawkins comes out of his office and tells Bryan and I to come in. Dr. Hawkins asks Mr. Lokkins if he had time to come in since he broke up the fight. After all of us are in the office, Dr. Hawkins tells us that Dr. Nunez is going to come in to help assess the situation.

"Dr. Nunez will bring in the video footage of the incident so don't try to lie about what occurred," says Principal Hawkins calmly.

Dr. Nunez is the assistant principal and she is mean to most students, yet every time I have an encounter with her, she is extremely nice. Although, she can be mean, all the guys are in love with her because she is young and pretty. Dr. Nunez comes in and gives Bryan and I a death stare. She projects the video footage of the incident on the screen.

"Alright, so before I show the footage of the incident, Dominic tell us what happened," she says.

"Bryan was talking about how good he was at football. I told him he was terrible just joking around. He started saying stuff as I walked away but I ignored him. I felt a hand touch my shoulder with an aggressive pull, I thought it was Bryan, so I just turned around and pushed. That's when I realized it was his sister. Bryan then went to go see if she was okay, but I thought he was running at me, so I flipped him over my back. This incident was all my fault, Bryan didn't do anything wrong except defending himself and swinging back as Mr. Lokkins pulled him back," I say calmly.

The facial expressions that everyone in the room had were blank and in shock, especially Bryan. He probably thought I was going to get him in trouble too. Dr. Nunez breaks the silence and plays the footage. Everything that I said had happened matched everything that was seen in the footage. Dr. Hawkins and Dr. Nunez had a long discussion of the events. When they turn around, Dr. Hawkins tells Bryan he has a one-hour office detention and is free to go home.

"Thank you for coming in Mr. Lokkins you're also free to go," says Nunez.

After they leave there is silence in the room for a couple of seconds.

"So, Dominic I'm only going to give you a one-hour detention for next year as well," says Dr. Hawkins.

"Really? I'm not suspended?" I ask in a surprising voice.

"No, because I know you just covered Bryan from getting in trouble," Dr. Hawkins says with a grin.

"How'd you know?"

"Bryan is a cocky punk and I have heard the things that have come out of his mouth. I also know you're an honor roll student," says Hawkins calmly.

"I'm really sorry this happened, it won't happen again," I say softly.

"Dr. Nunez here will walk you to the front as a precaution," says Dr. Hawkins.

I get up and walk out of the room. The school is pretty much empty since everyone has left for summer break. When we're walking to the front, Dr. Nunez asks me what my summer plans are. I tell her I'm not doing anything very exciting.

"From what I understand, your father went missing while visiting Sido eighteen years ago," Dr. Nunez says.

"Yes, all I want to know is what really happened to him and the others over the last two decades," I say.

"I want to know what happens in Sido as well so if I get a group together would you be willing to investigate Sido with us?"

When we get to the school doors, I look her in her eyes and ask her when.

"Tomorrow. Meet me at the family park at four o'clock to plan out the evening, then we'll start heading to Sido around eight."

"Alright, I'll be there," I say.

Dr. Nunez smiles and says she's glad, then turns around and heads back to her office. I walk out of the school in shock. Dr. Nunez just asked me to go with her to Sido, is this a dream? My whole walk home I am just completely startled. I then realize I told her that I'd go to Sido with her, would this be a mistake? When I get home my mom isn't there, and she is always here when I come home from school. I throw my stuff on the floor, turn the TV on, and lay on the couch. I watch the local news and the reporters urge people not to go to Sido. I close my eyes imagining what it would be like to go to Sido and what I would see. I open my eyes and the news reporter is standing in front of the electric fence talking about the disappearances. That's when I see a figure beyond the reporter, I look closer and that's when I realize who it is, I begin to shake and scream.

"Honey, honey! What's wrong?" My mom asks.

"I saw dad, he's alive," I say stuttering.

Then I realize I'm talking to my mom, she wasn't here when I got here, how is she here now? I never heard her come in.

"Dom, baby, what are you talking about? Of course, your dad is alive."

9

I begin shaking, what is she talking about? My dad is clearly gone, what's happening? Still shaking I hear a knock at the door. She opens the door and I hear,

"Hello babe, it's good to be home."

It's my dad, he came back. I jump up and look at the door, but no one is there. I turn around and run into a figure, that's all bloody. Instantly, my eyes shoot open. My heart is racing, but I take multiple deep breaths to calm myself down. I'm okay, it was just a dream, I tell myself. I look at the TV and the news reporter is standing in front of the electric fence. I tell myself, oh hell no, and shut it off immediately. Just after I turned it off, my mom walks in.

∞ ∞ ∞

I continue to watch TV, while my mom cooks dinner. It is only 4 o'clock but feels like forever since I left school. The dreams about my dad being alive happen so often that they don't even bother me anymore. I realize I have bigger problems, with the incident that happened earlier today at school.

Now all I can think about is Alyssa and if she is okay. Alyssa and I have always been close friends and I have liked her since junior high. It's also obvious she feels the same way about me as I feel about her. But now I don't even know if she wants anything to do with me. I know high school relationships are stupid and I shouldn't worry about them, but with her, she never fails to put a smile on my face. I try to think of different ways that I could apologize to her but everything I think about is cliché. Finally, I decide to just go talk to my mom about it, to see what she thinks.

I go into the kitchen and say, "Mom, today at school Bryan said something about Dad and I walked away, but as I was walking away I felt a hand on my shoulder, so I thought it was Bryan. I then snapped and shoved him, except it wasn't him, it was Alyssa. You know how I feel about Alyssa, I'd never hurt her but now I don't know how to apologize to her."

After I said this, I could see her eyes begin to water because she knew how bad I felt about this. She then takes a deep breath and sets what she's cooking off to the side.

"Come have a seat at the table to talk about this," my mom says softly.

I walk over to the table and have a seat next to my mom. We stare at each other for about ten seconds, then she finally breaks the silence.

"So how much trouble are you in with the school?" She asks.

"They only gave me a one-hour detention to serve at the beginning of next school year."

There was a big sigh of relief from my mom. I know she was thinking that I was going to be suspended and if that happens I'd lose a lot of honors and scholarship opportunities.

"Okay, well, that isn't the worst thing, but you're mainly just worried about how Alyssa is and if she'll ever talk to you again, right?" She asks calmly.

"Yes, I care about her so much, I'd never want to hurt her, but now I don't even know where we stand," I say tearing up.

"Well honey, the best thing to do is to explain what happened and your feelings about everything. I tell you what, after we eat dinner you can take my truck over to her house and apologize. She may forgive you and everything will be okay, or it may take her awhile before she can forgive you, but either way she will know you care," she says with a smile.

She then gets up and goes back to cooking dinner. I decide to go to my bedroom and get on my laptop. I listen to music, trying to get my mind off what happened. But eventually I throw my headphones across my room and start panicking. I can't stop thinking about Alyssa. Is she okay? Did her parents have to take her to the hospital? I can't get the image out of my head of the shocked look on her face after the incident happened.

After hours of doing nothing but worrying, my mom finally calls me for dinner. I walk out into the living room; the TV is still on the news. I then sit down at the table to eat my dinner. My mom is very old school, she fixes my plate and I must eat everything before I can excuse myself. Elbows stay off the table, chew with mouth closed, and talk at a minimum. I sit there with tears in my eyes as I finish up eating dinner. The tears are caused by the fear that when I go over there she will tell me to go away. I will be expecting the worst, hoping for the best. I make sure every crumb is gone, before I excuse myself.

"Thank you, Mom, for the amazing dinner," I say.

"Aw honey, come here."

I walk over to her, giving her a big hug, scared of what's to come.

"I love you," I say

"I love you too, sweetie."

"Now take my keys and go tell the girl how you feel," my mom says.

I take her keys and get in the '74 pickup. When I start the truck, it rattles for a while and then rumbles on. I back out of the driveway and along I go. While I'm driving fear starts to take over. I try to calm myself down by listening to music, but it was only making it worse. The drive to her house is only about ten minutes but it felt like the longest drive of my life. I begin to approach her house, but I suddenly stop. I can't do this, I tell myself.

My hands are shaking, and my anxiety starts to kick in. I pull myself together and continue towards the house. I pull up to the curb in front of the house and shut the truck off. I say a quick prayer. When I get out of the truck my legs feel like jelly. What if when I get to the door and she answers nothing comes out of my mouth? I take the slowest walk possible just trying to talk myself out of it, but my feet keep moving towards the house. I walk up the front steps onto the porch as the light comes on. I gently open the door but as I'm doing so, I see headlights coming towards me. I panic and look around. I run over behind a bush just a couple feet to my right.

The car pulls into the driveway slowly. Once the car stops I see Alyssa get out of the car. I squint my eyes and see a guy driving but I don't recognize him. I hear Alyssa say to the guy, "Thank you for a good time tonight," then she shuts the car door. My heart instantly drops. Who is this guy? Is it her boyfriend? To my knowledge I didn't think she had one. I decide not to approach her because she probably doesn't want to see or talk to me anyway. Heartbroken, I watch her walk up the steps into her house. Once the door closes I rush over to the truck in a stealthy manner, trying not to cause any commotion.

I quickly get in my truck, trying to start it, but it won't start. I rattle the key, hitting the steering wheel as if it's going to make a difference. That's when I see the porch light flicker on. "Oh shit," I say to myself. I see the door open and know I've been seen. Alyssa walks towards me, looks around, then walks back inside. I rattle the key once more and the truck rumbles as I drive off.

The drive home was a long and lonely drive. I sit in my driveway for a few minutes thinking about everything. Finally, I get out of the truck and walk up the steps to the door. I walk into my house without saying a word. I go straight to my bed and plop under the sheets, burying my face into the pillow with tears. Nothing can ever go right for me. I plug in my headphones and let the music wash away the events of the day.

# CHAPTER TWO

The morning sun rises as I lay there in my bed. I look out the window, listening to the birds' chirp. All I could do was stay in bed and wonder why any girl would like me. I'm not a confident guy nor good at talking to girls, but Alyssa is different. She makes me feel comfortable and tells me I'm cute, but I feel like she's just saying that to be nice. I feel that I'm too skinny, but she thinks I'm a perfect build for being six foot tall. Alyssa is a little shorter than me. Her and I playfully argue about the length of my hair and she thinks I should cut it a little shorter. The point is, she is the only girl that understands me and makes me feel worth anything. My mom comes in my room and looks at me.

"I didn't even hear you come in last night, how'd it go?" She asks.

"She wasn't home," I say in a slight stutter.

"Aw I'm sorry Hun, maybe you can try again later."

"Yeah, maybe."

I open the window to let the cool breeze come in. I stare out into the direction of the river. As I lie there in my bed, I think to myself, how peaceful everything looks. I get on my laptop and look up, "How to get things off your mind."

After minutes of researching, I conclude that I'm going to go for a walk after breakfast. Finally, I decide to get up and put some clothes on. Looking in the mirror, I part my hair off to the side. Then I go into the bathroom to brush my teeth. After I get all ready, I go into the kitchen where bacon, eggs, and toast are waiting for me. I fix my plate and take a seat at the table. I eat my food slowly, just enjoying the moment. After I finish, I rinse my plate off. I go find my mom to tell her I'm going to go for a walk. I go downstairs to see her piling boxes together. She has been packing boxes a lot lately as if were about to move. She just tells me she's trying to pack all my dad's stuff away because it brings back too many memories.

"Thanks for breakfast," I say.

"No problem Hun, was it good?"

"Of course it was, always is. Can I go for a quick walk to try to free my mind?" I ask hesitantly.

"Yes, but be back at a quarter until eleven."

"Alright, I love you," I say as I give her a hug.

"I love you too, sweetie"

I walk back upstairs to put some shoes on. I then walk out into the morning cool air. The river really makes for a nice breeze. I decide to walk towards the southeast end of the Ouachita River, where it's safe to go. I walk at a faster pace than usual just because I must be home at a certain time. The city looks like a ghost town as everybody is probably sleeping in since we no longer have school. It takes about forty-five minutes to get to the river by foot. As I approach the river, I hear multiple helicopters flying over. People say the helicopters are just a bunch of news stations from other places that want to cover the mystical mystery of Hot Springs. I can hear the river roaring ahead as I come closer to the wooded area. There is a slightly steep hill that I walk down so I can get closer to the water.

Once I get to the bottom there is a picnic table. I take a seat and stare at the clearest of waters. I take out some sketch paper and a charcoal pencil, drawing everything around me. Art is something that interests me, even though I know I can't draw. When I'm putting the finishing touches on, I hear footsteps approaching. When I look around, there is nothing. I swear this place can get creepy yet be so peaceful. It's about five until ten so I decide I better get going. Suddenly, I freeze at the returning sound of footsteps. I turn around and jump back at who I see. It's Alyssa. Wide eyed, I'm looking at Alyssa. I stare at her trying to speak but no words will come out. Finally, she breaks the silence.

"I saw you at my house last night," she says.

I almost choke on my own saliva when she says this, but I remain speechless.

"Why were you there?" She asks.

"Uh, I was going to apologize for what happened but then I saw you with another guy," I say softly.

"So? You can't apologize to me because you thought I was with someone else? If you were truly sorry it wouldn't matter what the circumstances were," she says in a feisty manner.

"Look, sorry, I just panicked, and I really am sorry about yesterday, I would never do anything to hurt you, Alyssa."

"I know you wouldn't, it was just an accident, that's why I'm glad I ran into you," she says.

My heart went from beating fast to calming down. She isn't mad like I thought she would be. I begin to relax.

"So, what are you doing out here?" I ask.

"Just come out here occasionally, for relaxation, what about you?"

"Trying to get my mind off things, I thought you'd never talk to me again."

"Dominic, it's okay."

"I don't feel okay, I just," I say stuttering.

"Just?" She asks.

"I really like and care about you so it's bothering me," I say with a frown.

She comes in closer and wraps her arms around me. It catches me off guard. Until this point, no one knew that I had a crush on her. I feel like I'm in a dream, yet it's a reality.

"Dom, I promise everything's okay. And guess what," she says.

"What?"

Alyssa looks up at me and smiles, "I really like you too and always have."

The butterflies start to happen. I was speechless, I didn't know what to say. All I could do was smile, while I stare into her beautiful sky-blue eyes. I run my hands through her long thick light brown hair and rest my hand on her cheek. Her and I are so close I can feel the warmth from her face and as I'm about to lean in to kiss her, we're interrupted by my phone ringing. Reluctantly pulling away, I look at my phone to see it's my mom calling so I quickly answer and when I glance up I can see the disappointment in Alyssa's eyes. I sigh as I feel the same way. When I get off the phone I ask Alyssa if I can walk her home.

"Of course," she smiles.

We walk up the hill as I hold onto her, to make sure she doesn't fall. When we get to the top, her and I start walking towards her house. I reach down and grab her hand. She grabs mine and just smiles. I felt lucky and happy.

"How's your head?" I ask

"It's fine, no concussion but how about we don't talk about it."

"Okay, can I ask you something?" I ask softly.

"Sure"

"So, you obviously know I was at your house last night to apologize to you, but who was the guy that brought you home?"

There was an awkward silence for a couple seconds, as she looks down at the ground.

"That was my friend, Spencer. He lives in Rockwell, but I look at him like a brother. He has known my family my whole life. If we become a thing, you have nothing to worry about, I promise."

"Oh okay, so do you want to become something?" I ask curiously.

"Yes, but we need to hang out more often," she says.

"Are you free for an adventure tonight?" I ask.

"Umm, what do you mean by adventure?"

"Dr. Nunez invited me to go with a group of people to visit Sido tonight and asked if I wanted to go. I mean I grew up without my dad because of that place, so I want to see what is really happening in Sido," I say.

"Yeah, I don't know about that. If I don't go, will you do me a favor?" She asks.

"Yes, anything."

"Please don't go, the only way I want you to is if I do. I don't want anything to happen to you. I want things to happen

21

between us. I don't want to lose you before I ever have you," she says.

I keep walking not knowing what to say. I really want to go, but she is right. What if I end up disappearing? It's not worth going anymore because now I have something I care about.

"Okay I won't go without you but please let me know as soon as possible whether you're going. Everyone is meeting at the family park across the street from the airport at four. That's where we are going to come up with a plan for the night. Then around eight, the departure for Sido will begin," I say.

She nods and the rest of the walk to her house was silent. The breeze fades as Alyssa and I walk further away from the river. Once I get Alyssa to her house, I look into her beautiful blue eyes.

"Please consider going tonight," I say.

"Dom, I want to go but it's scary."

"I know, but you have me to protect you."

"I'll think about it," she says laughing.

I go in for a kiss but just as my lips are about to touch hers, I hear a voice.

"Hey Dom, slow down young one," says Bryan from the house, chuckling.

Seriously, is this happening again? I think to myself. Feeling frustrated I turn around to see Bryan's face.

"Hey man, I'm really sorry about yesterday, you didn't have to cover my ass, but I truly appreciate it," says Bryan seriously.

"You're good, you can't change the past," I say.

It's not like I'm going to be best friends with him since he said some heartless things about my dad. But I gained a slight respect for him since he apologized.

"Anyways I got a call from Dr. Nunez a little while ago, talking about Sido tonight. She told me you're going. She invited me, but I wanted to make sure that's cool with you," Bryan says.

"No!" Alyssa jumps in. "Dom's not going without me!"

"Well just go sis, it'll be fun," Bryan says.

"Alright I'll go but you guys have to promise me the minute I want to leave, we leave," she exclaims.

"We promise," Bryan and I say.

"I'll see you tonight," I say to Alyssa.

She smiles and walks towards her house. It's already ten-forty. I practically run home because I know every minute I'm late, my ass is mine.

∞ ∞ ∞

I get home around eleven. I walk in the door and immediately my mom is waiting. She clears her throat for a good five seconds.

"You're fifteen minutes late," says my mom.

"Yes, I know, I'm sorry," I say.

"So, why were you late?"

23

"I ran into Alyssa and we talked things out, then I took her home. There, I saw Bryan and he apologized. They want me to hangout tonight," I say.

"Wow! I'm happy things worked out. Where do they want to hangout and when?"

"Leave around three-thirty, I'm just going to go have dinner with them and play card games all night," I say, lying.

"Okay sounds good, you can take my truck. I don't need it tonight," she says.

I walk off to my room. The day goes by like the hands of a clock. Throughout the day, I can't stop thinking about earlier with Alyssa. Lying there, I'm anxious about the night. What if these are my final hours laying in this bed? What if when I tell my mom goodbye, it's the last time I see her? Is all this worth it? Will I just become father like son, both gone? Thoughts racing through my mind, but when the clock hits three-thirty, I'm ready to go. I've been waiting for this moment and now it's time to take advantage of the opportunity. I pack together a bag that contains food, knives, extra clothes, etc. I throw the bag onto my back and tell my mom goodbye for what could be the last time.

"Why are you taking a bag?" My mom asks.

"I just threw in some games and movies in the bag, to keep us entertained for the night," I say.

"Oh, okay. Have fun honey, don't do anything you're not supposed too, I love you."

"I love you too, Mom."

I grab the keys off the table. I walk out the door and turn around to see my house, for what may be the last time. I throw the bag in the passenger seat and start the drive to the family park. The traffic is moderate for the time of day. I turn onto airport road and continue down for a couple of minutes. I turn onto the road that takes me to the meeting spot. When I pull up I see Dr. Nunez and a couple others. I get out of the rusty truck and approach Dr. Nunez.

"Hey Dominic, is Bryan and Alyssa coming?" Dr. Nunez asks in excitement.

"Yes, they're supposed to be."

"Alright good, I'd like you to meet a few people."

There were three young people standing there. Two girls on the left and one guy to my right.

"So Dominic, this is Kyra, Aaliyah, and William," she says.

"Nice to meet you guys," I say awkwardly.

Dr. Nunez goes on to tell me that Kyra is a nurse at St. Vincent, the local hospital. Aaliyah is in the music industry and despite dropping out of high school, she has been successful. Lastly, William is Dr. Nunez's older brother.

"Once Bryan and Alyssa show up we'll get started," says Nunez.

After about ten minutes of small talk, Bryan and Alyssa show up. Bryan gets out of his Mustang, walking up with a cocky demeanor.

"Damn Dr. Nunez, looking fine as ever," says Bryan with a smirk.

I couldn't help but laugh, he really didn't care.

"Bryan, stop! Lookup!" Nunez exclaims.

But Bryan continued to look Nunez up and down, until Dr. Nunez slapped him. This caught everyone off guard, especially Bryan.

"Okay, okay, Doctor," says Bryan smiling. "It looks like you're into that discipline stuff."

"Get lost, I hope you disappear tonight," she says joking.

It gets very quiet cause we all know it's possible all of us can be gone in an instant tonight.

"Hey Hun," Alyssa says to me with a smile.

"You scared?" I ask.

"A little bit, but I have you to protect me."

"Wherever you go, I go. We're doing this together." I say.

She smiles. Dr. Nunez rolls out a large map of the city. All over the map, there are points that indicate certain locations and directions. Dr. Nunez then hands us all an eight by eleven version of the map just in case we forget something or get lost.

"Okay, I've been working on this mission to Sido for the last couple of months. One of my mom's friends husband went missing in Sido long ago. I promised my mom that I would get answers for her friend one day. That one day happens to be today," says Nunez.

Dr. Nunez hands us all a walkie talkie.

"These will last the whole night. They communicate within a one-mile radius. We have to have good communication," she exclaims.

If I had to say one thing about Dr. Nunez, she knew what the hell she was doing. She didn't come to play around, she was prepared and ready.

"Also, here is a compass for each one of you, it'll be easy to get lost. Make sure you don't lose this because you don't want to be lost in the middle of a place where people go missing. I believe if we're smart, we can make it out. We'll have two cameras to film it all. Not only can we find out what happens, but we can present it to the world and get a lot of money," she says.

The more she talked, the more I became intrigued into wanting to go to Sido. This was the craziest thing any of us had done. My stomach becomes very queasy, but I know if everything turns out okay, it'll be worth it. She then starts talking to us about the map.

"So, here we are. We are going to drive from here to just past Lakeshore Drive. You're going to take a right on Weston Drive towards the harbor. Once on Stearns Point Drive, take a right and go onto Owen's Point. From there we will walk to where the fence is located, which is just in front of Myrick Lane. All Sido used to be was full of houses until the government destroyed them all. Now the time has come to unveil the mystery. Like I've said, I planned this for months, so I already have a small underground tunnel that will lead us into Sido. Obviously, there are only guards on the outside of the fence but from our point of entry, there should be none. If you look at the map, I have Sido split off into a clock. Based on your compass you will be able to tell where you're at. So, if your compass is pointing northeast, you're in the one to two o'clock range. If you need to get out then just head nine o'clock to get back to the tunnel," says Nunez.

All of this is just becoming more surreal. I look over at Alyssa and her face is as white as snow. I reach over and grab her hand to let her know I'm always going to be by her side.

"Please never let go," she says.

"I won't," I say.

Dr. Nunez goes on and on talking about what needs to happen. There is one part I'm quite skeptical of. She said we're going to split up into two groups. One group consisting of Alyssa, Nunez, Bryan, and myself. The other group will be the three others that came. I'm going into Sido with the mindset of expecting the worst. Sadly, I'm sure at least one of us will not make it out tonight. All of a sudden, a wave of fear overcomes me and I find myself frantically shouting, "I can't go, I don't want to do this anymore."

Everyone looks at me and stares. Dr. Nunez comes up to me, softly grabbing my shoulders.

"Yes you can Dominic, for your dad and to get the answers you so desperately want."

She was right, I came to find answers. I was just running away in fear. I need to stay and fight through my fears. I roll up the map and tell Alyssa to ride with me. I look around as this may be the last time I see the city lights.

# CHAPTER THREE

The clock strikes eight as it's time for the departure to Sido. Alyssa and I hop in my truck. The truck gives the rumbling sound. I look at Alyssa as she just blankly stares out the window. I turn back onto Airport road, then continue down highway seventy.

Once I see the sign for Weston road, I take a right, to go down Stearns Point. When I near Owens Point, I can see the Fence in the distance, secured by forces. Luckily, I'm far enough away to where they won't see me coming in. The adrenaline flows faster and faster as I stay right and down to Owens Point. Waiting for me is Dr. Nunez and her crew, with Bryan right behind me. I dim the headlights and park in the grass off to the side. Once I step out of the truck, I know there's no turning back. I grab the tools Nunez provided us and grab my bag. I help Alyssa out of the truck as she is still pale.

"Alyssa listen, it's all going to be okay," I say, hugging her tightly.

"I'm scared, I don't want anything bad to happen and bad things always happen here," she says trembling.

"Alyssa look at me, nothing bad is going to happen but you have to trust me, do you trust me?"

"I trust that you think everything is going to be okay even though we both know this is a stupid idea."

I take a deep breath and close my eyes. When I do this, something scary happens. My whole life flashes before my eyes. My heart starts beating at a fast pace. I count slowly to ten and open my eyes.

"If you die, I die. I'm not going to let anything happen to you. You will always come before me, no matter what," I say.

"No stop! I'm not worth any of that"

"Shh," I say. "You're worth everything."

I grab her hand and walk over to Dr. Nunez's car. She tells all of us to grab each other's hand, close our eyes, and kneel to the ground. She then speaks,

"Our Father, which art in heaven, hallowed be thy name. Thy Kingdom come. Thy will be done on earth, as it is in heaven. Give us this day our daily bread. And forgive us our trespasses, as we forgive them that trespass against us. And lead us not into temptation, but deliver us from evil. For thine is the kingdom, the power, and the glory, For ever and ever. Amen."

"Alright, make sure you have everything and follow me to the tunnel," says Nunez.

Everyone follows Nunez to the tunnel. It was about a ten-minute walk in the tall grass. We were told to watch out for snakes, but none were seen. Once we arrive at the tunnel, I notice the fence is still a good thirty yards away.

"Alright one by one crawl through the tunnel, be sure to stay quiet," says Nunez

"Screw this, I'm claustrophobic," says Bryan.

"It's honestly not that bad Bryan, don't be a girl," says Nunez.

I make sure Alyssa goes in front of me, so I can make sure nothing bad happens to her. The tunnel is very small, as I feel sandwiched from all sides and can't move anywhere but forward.

"Dom, I'm starting to panic, I feel like I can't breathe," Alyssa says whispering.

"Babe, I'm right behind you, everything's going to be okay," I say.

I try to stay calm for Alyssa, but quite honestly, I'm starting to panic too. I close my eyes and just keep crawling. I can tell we're getting closer to the end of the tunnel because I can feel the breeze getting cooler. I open my eyes and that's when I see the end of the tunnel. Alyssa crawls out of the hole and I follow. I look at my watch and we were only crawling for four minutes, but it felt like hours. I was just glad I could finally breathe and not feel so condensed. I then realize that I'm in Sido. I look around at the familiar sightings I remember from years ago when it was open to the public. Once everyone makes it out of the tunnel, we're all breathless. Bryan is standing off to the side mumbling curse words at the ground.

"Welcome to Sido," says Nunez.

"Go get lost Dr. Nunez, I thought my life was ending in the tunnel," says Bryan angrily.

For the first time in my life, I wanted to go give Bryan a high five. Dr. Nunez never told us how small she made the tunnel. She just expected us to be okay with it. We stand in silence in the middle of Sido where people disappear, like it's no big deal.

"Uh, can we get going because my stomach is starting to feel weird just standing here," I say.

"Okay, let's go. William, take your group and cover the west side of Sido. Remember to be constantly filming every footstep," says Nunez.

She then looks at me in silence for a couple of seconds.

"Dom, are you ready?" Nunez asks.

"I guess, let's get it over with," I say.

Alyssa, Bryan, Nunez, and I will cover the east side of Sido. We walk around as if nothing bad happens here. Within five minutes of being there, weird things start to occur. Screams of people could be heard from afar.

"William, everything okay?" Nunez asks through the walkie talkie.

"Affirm, just a little creepy," William says.

Sido was the exact definition of creepy. I look at Alyssa and she looks at me with a frightened look on her face. I grab her hand and pull her to my side. I wanted to reassure her with a kiss, but I felt like this was a weird place to experience our first kiss. As we keep walking strange noises occurred. I look at my compass and figure out we're in the 2 o'clock range. Dr. Nunez has been recording the whole time but nothing crazy enough has happened.

"Hey Dr. Nunez, you know I'm eighteen, it's not illegal," says Bryan bringing some laughter.

"Keep dreaming honey. We would have to make it out of here before anything," says Nunez joking.

I realize Bryan really isn't a bad guy, despite his persona of being arrogant, cocky, and a jock. He has enlightened the mood of the night with his confidence towards Nunez. My legs begin to hurt from walking. I notice something in the corner of my eye. I slowly turn to see a figure coming towards me. Startled, I let out a slight scream just to realize it was a bat flying by. Embarrassed by my reaction, Alyssa sees the look on my face and pulls me closer as I hear Bryan say laughing, "who's protecting who?"

"Dom, calm down it's okay," says Alyssa.

I become jittery and shaky. At this point, I just want to turn around and leave, but my conscience tells me no. We make it to the river bank where the cool breeze sweeps across my face, while I stare at the flowing water.

"What the hell? How do people go missing? Nothing has happened," says Nunez.

That's when we look around and notice something unusual. Bryan is gone, he was here and now he's nowhere to be seen. Just when we thought nothing was going to happen, it did. In the distance, I hear sounds of ATV's and dirt bikes. People aren't just vanishing, people are getting abducted. That's when I hear a humming sound above me and there are thousands of drones floating above. One of the drones drops off a rolled piece of paper. I unroll the paper and begin to read.

"Dominic get everyone out, it's too dangerous here. You have people that care about you, so just run and don't look back. You're not meant to be here yet."

A state of confusion takes control of my mind. My instincts take over, so I stick the paper in my pocket, grab Alyssa's hand and begin to run. Nunez follows behind us but fell trying to keep up. At first, I wanted to go back and help Dr. Nunez, but I tell myself to keep going and all of this was her fault anyways. I reach into my pocket and grab the compass. The sounds of the ATV's and dirt bikes get louder. The sounds of the drones were following. There was only one thing I knew and that was to not stop running. Without looking back Alyssa and I come to the tunnel. I have her crawl through first. When I go to get in I feel a shot to the neck. I look to my left to see a human figure, but my vision was too blurry to make out who it is. I feel the figure pick me up as the voice of a man spoke.

"It's going to be alright, you'll wake up in the hospital tomorrow," says the voice.

∞ ∞ ∞

I hear a constant beeping sound. My eyes slowly open as I gain consciousness. I could see that there were people sitting around me.

"Where am I?" I ask in a soft, raspy voice.

There was no response from anyone as if I couldn't be heard. My vision was too foggy to see who was around me. I take a couple deep breaths and yell.

"Where the hell am I?"

The people become silent. I may not have been able to tell who was around me but I could see the figures freeze.

"Dom, oh my god honey, are you okay?" A familiar voice asks.

Even though the voice sounded familiar I still couldn't figure out who it was. But whoever it is wouldn't stop grabbing my hand.

"Who are you?" I ask.

The hand froze without an inch of movement. It was as if whoever I was speaking to couldn't breathe anymore.

"Dominic, I'm your mom. I know you just woke up so everything probably is confusing right now," she says.

"Mom? I don't have a mom, she went missing when I was young, I want Dad," I say.

The woman proclaiming to be my mom starts yelling for a nurse.

Nurse? I think. That's when I realize I'm in a hospital. Truthfully, I didn't even know who I was. My vision starts to clear up and I see about four people in my room. I didn't know who anyone was.

"Yes ma'am, what's wrong?" I hear the nurse whisper.

"He doesn't know who I am, and believes his father is still alive," says my so-called mom.

The nurse comes in and asks me some questions. She asks about my past that I vaguely can remember. The more she talks the more I start to remember.

"This was expected, yesterday we ran blood tests when he first got admitted and found Diazepam in his system. Diazepam is a drug that gets injected into your system and can cause paranoia, suicidal thoughts, and can impair memory. It's used for anxiety but the dosage he accumulated was more than a fair amount. The good thing is his memory is already starting to come back slowly, which means eventually everything will be normal again but it's just going to take time," says the Nurse.

My mom takes a deep breath and relaxes as the nurse speaks. The more time that passes by, the more I can remember.

"Where's Alyssa?" I ask my mom.

"Well Bryan disappeared, so the family is grieving," she says.

Suddenly, I see a young woman come in my room. I squint as I recognize the woman. Then it hit me, it's Dr. Nunez. Then I wonder why she's here because the last time I saw her was in Principal Hawking's office.

"May I help you?" My mom addresses Nunez.

"Yeah, I'm the assistant principal at Dominic's school and heard about the incident, so I wanted to check up on his well-being," says Nunez.

"Oh wow, thanks for coming. He's doing better, just has some memory issues," my mom says with a glare.

"May I talk to him alone?"

"For?"

"I'm sure you heard of the little scuffle on the last day of school, just wanted to speak with him in private about the situation."

"Okay. He may not remember, but go ahead," says my mom as she and the others leave the room.

Dr. Nunez walks around the room in silence. I notice she has cuts all over her body as if she fell. For me, I was in a state of confusion why she would want to talk about the scuffle as I'm lying in a hospital.

"So, do you remember anything from the other night and understand why you're in the hospital right now?" She asks calmly.

"No ma'am, what happened?" I say confused.

She takes a deep breath and speaks, "I was going to visit Sido with a couple of friends. When we pulled up, Alyssa was standing there freaking out. She told me you were shot in the neck and taken by a figure that appeared to be human. She also told me that her brother, Bryan, was also taken. She said it was your idea to go see what happens in Sido. Anyways my friends and I put her in my vehicle, to take her home. After we dropped her off, I got a phone call from your phone. It was a female voice saying you were in the hospital."

"So? What's all that supposed to mean?" I ask.

"Well, more than likely, whoever was behind that call knows what's happening in Sido. Now, I had one of my friend's ping where the phone call was coming from. It came from this very hospital, and now I know who's voice it is. But since this hospital is secured with cameras, I want you to ask to see the footage, so you can find out the truth," she says.

My mind begins to race with so many thoughts. Why would I want to visit the most dangerous place on earth? Nothing made sense to me. Nunez's story especially made absolutely no sense. What are the odds of her actually being there as if she knew something was going to happen? Although on the other hand, the footage from the cameras could reveal the biggest secret to date.

Why wouldn't she just tell me who's voice it was? Then I think, probably because I wouldn't believe her. Just like how I don't believe her right now.

"Dom, everything is one big lie. Everything you were told while growing up was just one big fat lie," she says.

Memories of the chilling night start hitting me. I drove to the family park to meet Nunez and her friends for a plan on how the night was going to go. Bryan and Alyssa also met us there. Sido was divided into a clock. Nunez had a tunnel to enter Sido, which was a very tight space. Alyssa, Bryan, Nunez, and I took the east half of Sido. Nothing strange was happening until Bryan disappeared and drones swarmed over us. Sounds of dirt bikes and ATV's could be heard from afar. Then a note, but I can't remember what the note said. All I know is I ran, then Nunez fell but Alyssa and I didn't stop. Alyssa jumps in the tunnel first and when I was about to crawl into the tunnel, I was shot. A strong man picked me up and carried me for about five minutes. Then everything became bright and people were talking about airplanes. Then the man handed me off to a woman, then I woke up here.

"Wait! You're lying! This is all your fault, I remember everything. How did you make it out?" I ask.

She glances at me and becomes very pale. She opens the door, looks at me and says one word, "Footage."

"Mom!" I yell.

She rushes in there quickly.

"What's wrong honey?"

"Dr. Nunez is connected to Sido somehow. She was there that night, it was all her idea. Then when I was running away, she fell. She purposely fell, so everything could play out the way it did," I exclaim.

"Honey, I don't think you know what you're talking about. I think she just came in here to make you believe something that never happened."

"Mom, no! I was there. There were drones everywhere, it really happened."

"Sweetie, I think you just need some rest," she says.

She doesn't believe me. She was told something else happened to me. But what? What could explain the drug being in my system that slightly impaired my memory? I just roll over and fall back to sleep.

When I wake up it's dark outside. I look up at the clock as it reads seven fifty-nine. I just look up until the clock strikes eight. As this happens my body becomes very chilled as I realized that was the time that we departed for Sido. I lay there lonely in a room full of darkness. I feel something scratching my lower back, so I roll over to find a folded piece of paper. I open the paper slowly. There are words on the paper that read, "I'm sorry I lied, but ask to see VIDEO FOOTAGE!" The note was from Dr. Nunez. I lay there and think of what she said. I decide the video footage might be a clue to something happening within Sido and whoever brought me here

41

may be able to explain everything. I buzz in a nurse, so I can ask to go to the camera room.

"Is everything okay?" The nurse asks.

"Yeah, can I see footage of who brought me here?"

"Oh no sorry, I don't have the authorization to do that."

"Can you somehow get authorization to let me see?"

"I'm sorry I can't but I can go find out the name of the person that brought you here."

"Okay fine," I say frustrated.

The nurse was gone for a good ten minutes. I didn't think she was coming back but she finally comes back in.

"Okay, I was out there talking about you wanting to see the cameras and one of our tech employees said she'd take you to see the footage. On another note, the person that signed you in was Alyssa Washburn. I'll get a wheelchair to take you to the video room," she says.

Alyssa? I think. There's no way Alyssa brought me here. She doesn't even drive, that's impossible. The nurse comes back in and lifts me into a wheelchair. We get in the elevator and go to the floor that the video room is located. She opens the door and tells me she'll be waiting outside. I roll in the room to find Dr. Nunez sitting in front of the screens. Immediately I turn around to leave but then I tell myself to just go and find out.

"Hey Dom, you ready to watch?" Nunez asks.

"Sure."

I roll next to her in my wheelchair, as she hits play. At first, there was nothing, but then I see who the woman is. Chills rush through my body as I become frozen. I whisper only one word to myself.

"Mom."

# CHAPTER FOUR

It's Saturday morning, as I look outside it's gloomy. I roll over to see what time it was as the clock reads, nine thirty-two. My stomach grumbles so I buzz for a nurse. The nurse walks in with a slight smile.

"Good morning," she says.

"Good morning," I reply.

"Ready for breakfast?"

"Yes."

She brings in a plate of food, then sets it on the table. The breakfast here is very stale but it's food. I lift my bed upright as I begin to eat.

"Thanks," I say.

She smiles and walks out of the room. While I sit there eating my breakfast, I remember what happened last night. I decide to sleep on the idea that my mom may have something to do with this. The only thing I keep asking myself is what kind of assistant principal leads kids they barely know into a dangerous area? I feel like Dr. Nunez has dark secrets that she is not willing to let out. But the fact is my mom did bring me here and that almost seems quite impossible. Why would she sign her name under Alyssa? I guess once I get out of the hospital I can maybe figure it all out. The nurse comes back in and checks a couple things.

"Dominic, you look all good, your mom is on her way and once she gets here, you're free to go," says the nurse.

In the meantime, I just watch TV until she gets here. I flip through the channels as I come across a local news station. I sit there focused with my eyes bulging out of my head.

"One arrested in connection with the disappearance of eighteen-year-old Bryan Washburn and injured seventeen-year-old Dominic Wilkerson, the person in connection with the two teenagers name has not yet been released but the authorities did say this person was an administrator at Hot Springs High School," says a news reporter.

Dr. Nunez is the first person that comes into mind. She got caught, a sense of excitement is felt throughout my body. I turn the TV off, laying there until my mom gets here. The nurse comes in and hands me some clothes my mom brought. She helps me to the restroom, so I can change. After I change my clothes she helps me into a wheelchair. Finally, I get to go home I tell myself. She leads us down the elevator and out the front doors where my mom is waiting for me. My mom gets out of car and helps me into the passenger seat. My mom talks to the nurse for a couple minutes and I just lay my head back in the seat.

"Dom," I hear a whisper.

I look back and it's Dr. Nunez. No way, how is she here? What is going on I ask myself.

"Get away from me! What's going on?"

"Calm down, I'm just a part of your imagination right now," she says.

"Bullshit!" I exclaim.

My mom must have seen me talking because she gets in the car quickly.

"Honey, who are you talking too?"

"Huh? No one."

"Hmm, are you sure you're alright?"

"Yes Mom, let's go home now."

The ride home was quiet. All I could think about is how my mom is connected to Sido. My biggest regret of my life was going to Sido the other night. I let animosity dictate my actions and now I'm paying for that decision. It feels like forever since I last seen Alyssa. Honestly, I miss her a lot. The thought of Bryan disappearing gets to me because it could've all been prevented. It all goes back to the presentation that we are given before summer break began. When we near my house, I see the media surrounding my driveway. At first, I was very confused, but soon came to the realization that I made it out of Sido without disappearing. In fact, Alyssa, Dr. Nunez, and I all made it out. But what happened to the people Dr. Nunez brought? Did they make it out? Although, I feel like the only reason Dr. Nunez made it out safely is because she's connected to the disappearances somehow. So, if she is, would she make her own brother disappear? All these questions unknown.

There is a couple of cops at the end of my driveway that clear the crowds of reporters. My mom opens the garage and pulls in while quickly shutting the garage behind us. She looks at me and then gets out of the car.

"They've been here all morning since the news broke," says my mom calmly.

I just look at her with a blank stare while walking inside. She comes storming in through the basement door that connects to the garage.

"Dominic! What the hell is going on?"

Again, I look at her and walk off to my room, shutting my door behind me. Next thing I know my mom is busting through the door.

"How disrespectful!"

I cut her short of her sentence.

"Disrespectful? I think I have every right not to respect you."

"Excuse me?"

I see her coming at me about to slap me but as she's about to do so, I say three words.

"What's your connection?"

She stops almost immediately. She stands there in confusion.

"Connection to what?"

"Sido, I seen the footage showing that you took me to the hospital."

She tries to open her mouth to only remain speechless.

"Dom, I can explain. I promise I'm not connected."

"Well I'm all ears for whatever you have to say."

"Come sit down at the kitchen table," she says.

I walk very slowly into the kitchen. It's sad that I can't even trust my own mom. I sit down on a chair across from her. She clears her throat, acting a little nervous.

"So, after you left, I became very suspicious. But I just kept telling myself you weren't doing anything you shouldn't be doing. Around nine o'clock that night I sent you a text asking how everything was going. A message was sent back saying, "Come get me." The message had a location tag. It said you were located at the "Hamilton Harbor Resort" which is right next to Sido. So, I knew you were probably in trouble. Then I called my friend Karen to come pick me up since you had the truck. When we arrived at the resort you were just lying in the parking lot with a note that said, "Hospital ASAP!" So, I rushed you to the hospital."

I sit there quietly for a couple minutes. As much as I want to believe her, I don't. To me the story sounds fabricated.

"Why did you write down Alyssa's name on the sign in sheet?" I ask.

"Huh? I never signed into the hospital."

"Mom, the nurse told me you signed in as Alyssa, you don't have to lie."

"Honey, I'm not lying. I rushed you in and they immediately took you to a room. There was no time to sign in."

"Well, obviously you did, and now you got caught so you don't want to admit it."

"Dom, there is nothing to admit because I never touched a sign in sheet."

"Whatever, I'm done," I say, walking away.

∞ ∞ ∞

I go in my room and get all the things I need. I find a new backpack and stuff everything into it. I forget the media is swarming my driveway, so I can't leave in plain sight. I get a hoodie out of my closet and pull the hood over my head. I then put on a hat and put a pair of sunglasses on. I do anything to make myself look less recognizable. In the basement there is a sliding door that leads to a small wooded area. When I have everything together, I sneak down into the basement. Then I quietly open and close the sliding door. Once out, I walk through the wooded area for a little bit. Eventually

49

I find the street and work my way to Central Avenue. From there I see a McDonald's down the street and know I can get free Wi-Fi, since I ran out of data. When I'm within a few hundred feet of the McDonalds, I hear a voice.

"Dom."

I look around, but I don't see anyone.

"Dom!"

This time when I turn around I see Dr. Nunez hiding in the bushes.

"Dr. Nunez?" I say.

She comes out of the bushes, still with scratches everywhere from Sido.

"Let's go inside," she says.

I sit down across from her, filled with hate towards her.

"Are you stalking me?" I ask.

"Dom, I'm here for your safety."

"Screw you, what assistant principal leads a group of students into a dangerous place?"

"Me, because answers need to be known. Sido is bigger than all of us and in a year Sido will no longer be a mystery."

No longer be a mystery? What is she talking about? The fact is Sido has been a mystery for the last eighteen years and will always be for years to come.

"Dominic listen, you can't trust the people closest to you, literally no one."

50

"Oh okay. So, I should trust everything you say?" I ask angrily.

"Dominic I'm looking out for you. I'm trying to keep you from evil and the lies. I was sent here to look after you."

"By who?" I ask curiously.

"I can't say, but the one thing I need from you is to trust me."

"You know what Dr. Nunez. Go screw yourself, get out of my life!" I yell.

She sits there with a blank gaze.

"Okay then." she says leaving with tears in her eyes.

She takes a couple steps away, then she comes back to hand me an envelope.

"Maybe this will get you to trust me."

The date on the back of the envelope marks, December 11, 1997. Also on the back it says, "Written for Stephanie Wilkerson and my unborn son, Dominic Wilkerson." The envelope has already been torn open. In the envelope there is a folded piece of paper. I quickly unfold the paper. The paper reads,

*"My darling Stephanie and Dominic,*

*I'm sorry if this is the last you hear from me. Stephanie, I love you both so much and I hope to see you soon. Dominic, if you happen to grow up without me just know you always have your mom. You probably will think you'll have to live in wonder your whole life but with time my disappearance and the other*

*disappearances will be solved and explained. Sido is bigger than all of us. There will be theories, but put those theories to rest because they're not true. Don't get curious and come here, it's not worth it and you'll eventually find out the truths. I can tell you we're not the only ones. I plan on coming back in about fifteen years to reveal the truths. If you don't hear from me within fifteen years just know more than likely I'm no longer here. The world is becoming more and more dangerous and I fear for what is to come. With this letter I trust everything you read will stay confidential because if this gets out, you risk the lives of others. I hope to see you soon.*
*~Loving Husband and Father"*

    I catch myself shedding tears after I read this. I didn't even know how to process what I just read. I conclude that he is no longer alive because he never came. Deep down I have hope that maybe everything got pushed back and he will come soon. But the fact is, Sido is not what everyone thinks it is. I can only come up with two theories. The first theory is that if you disappear then you don't die and get held as a prisoner for trespassing. Or when you disappear the people behind this kill you and dispose your body. Then I think, I was captured and neither of these things happened. I was released and woke up in a hospital. This leaving me with thousands of questions and a state of confusion. I notice another folded up piece of paper in the envelope, so I unfold the paper.

*"Trust me? If you want to find out answers meet me at the high school at five. I can answer only some of your questions. I want to help you Dom. You just need to trust me." ~Nunez*

I don't understand why Dr. Nunez would ever think I'd trust her again. Everything that comes out of her mouth is just one big lie. I connect to the Wi-Fi, so I can message Alyssa. I then decide to call her instead.

"Hey."

"Hey babe, it's good to hear your voice. Is everything okay?"

"Yes. I need to talk to you, meet at Pizza Hut off Central?"

"Yeah, I'll be there in a few," she says.

I walk across Central to the Pizza Hut. This is where everyone comes to hangout after sporting events. Once there I get a small pizza. I wait there for a little bit until her mom drops her off. When she sees me, she runs to me and I hug her tightly. She has tears in her eyes.

"I missed you," I say.

"I missed you too."

We take a seat as I sit next to her.

"I'm sorry about your brother," I say.

"It's been tough. Bryan and I were close all our lives. I just can't believe one day he's here and then all the sudden, he's gone. Nothing seems real right now," she says choking back tears.

I sit there for a few minutes awkwardly. I then reach my hands into my pocket as I grab the envelope. I hand her the folded-up letter that my dad wrote.

"This is why I wanted to see you, because Bryan might be alive and okay," I say trying to give her hope about Bryan.

She unfolds the paper and begins to read the letter. At first, she was very calm and collective and when she got further along she started shedding tears of her own. After a couple of minutes, she sets the paper on the table.

"I'm so sorry," she says.

"It's okay, I never knew him and never will. But I believe there is a big issue occurring where we live and we have to figure out what's happening," I say.

"How are you going to figure out what's happening? You can't risk going back into Sido."

"It's the only way," I say.

"Dom please don't, just let it go. Your dad even says in the letter that eventually the truths will come out, don't risk going back."

"Why shouldn't I go back? I lost my dad, my mom is a liar, and Dr. Nunez is connected to all of this."

"Huh? What did your mom do? Wasn't Dr. Nunez charged with what happened?"

"Dr. Nunez has been following me. I saw her today and she wants me to meet her tonight, at the school to answer any questions

I have. She's the one that gave me this letter and says her duty is to protect me. Also, my mom took me to the hospital the other night and signed in as you. All I have is you now," I say.

"Dominic. Your mom didn't take you to the hospital, I did," she says.

I sit there with my jaw dropped. "What the hell is going on?" I think. Chills rush throughout my body as I'm in shock.

"What are you talking about?" I ask.

"When I was climbing into the small tunnel, I heard a noise behind me. So, I looked back and you were lying on the ground with a tranquilizer injected into your neck. I looked around but there was no one. I tried picking you up, but I couldn't. So, I told Dr. Nunez's brother, William, over the walkie talkie what happened, so he rushed over. He picked you up and we got you out of Sido. William then gave me the keys to his car and told me to get you to the hospital quickly. He went back for Kyra and Aaliyah. I then asked for assistance when I got there and they told me to sign in. Then they lifted you onto a hospital bed and that was the last time I seen you until now."

I sit there for a moment. My heart is beating out of my chest. I clearly seen video footage of my mom taking me into the hospital. What is happening? Alyssa's story is the only one that makes any sense which means again Dr. Nunez lied to me and so did my mom.

"That's the truth?" I ask.

"I promise."

I still wonder what school administrator was charged with the connection of what happened to Bryan and I. I want Dr. Nunez gone. She's only made my life worse in the past week. I wish I could go back to the last day of school and tell her no when she asked about finding out what happened to my dad.

"I have a plan," I say.

"What's that?"

"I want you to go to the police station and tell them Dr. Nunez is in connection with everything that has happened. She's the one that led us into Sido. Then tonight, when I go meet with her I can hook up a mic to my shirt, so they hear everything. Once she confesses everything, then the police can swarm in on her and put her where she belongs."

"Are you sure you want to do that?" Alyssa asks.

"Positive."

"When are you supposed to meet her?"

"Five. What time is it right now?"

"Three, so we need to get going."

"Can you call your mom to take us?" I ask.

"Let me see."

Alyssa gets a hold of her mom and says she'll take us. After about ten minutes of waiting, her mom finally arrives. We take a seven-minute drive until we reach Grand Avenue, where the police station is located. When there, Alyssa jumps out of the car. After several minutes Alyssa waves at me to come inside. An officer tells me to have a seat.

"So, Alyssa here told me everything, but I have some bad news," says the officer.

"What's that?" I ask.

"About twenty minutes ago a call was made that a body was found in the creek by the golf course. Sadly, the body found was Mrs. Nunez's. No details are being released and we'd like if you didn't say much to anyone until the whole story develops," he says.

My heart just sinks. I can't believe she's dead. I know I hated her, but she was the only way to get answers to my questions, even if I thought she was a liar. I would never want this to happen to anyone. I feel myself starting to have a breakdown.

"I need to go, thanks officer," I say.

I get up, then walk out and get into the car.

"Is everything okay?" Alyssa's mom asks.

"Yes," Alyssa says.

I lean over and whisper to Alyssa, "Can I stay with you for a while?"

Alyssa looks over and smiles, "I'd love that."

"Would it be okay if Dominic stayed with us for a while?" Alyssa asks her mom.

Alyssa's mom was a little hesitant at first, but said she would talk to Alyssa's dad to make sure it was okay. I grab Alyssa's hand and the rest of the ride home was silent.

# CHAPTER FIVE

When I get to Alyssa's, I fall asleep. When I wake up it's nine o'clock at night. I find myself on the couch all alone. I look up to find that the news is on the television. The breaking story is captioned, "Hot Springs High School Assistant Principal Body is Found in Creek." I wonder to myself what happened after she left McDonald's. It's only a matter of time before the authorities question me since I was the last person to see Dr. Nunez alive. I can hear Alyssa's parents having a little scuffle in the kitchen. As I pay more attention to their conversation I know they're arguing about me staying here. Slowly, I walk into the kitchen and they immediately stop arguing.

"I don't want this to be a problem, I'll find somewhere else to stay," I say sadly.

Her parents just look at each other without exchanging a word.

"Dominic, right?" Her dad asks with a slight east coast accent.

"Yes, sir."

"Let's go talk downstairs."

Her dad walks out of the kitchen as I follow. I become very scared and shaky. Honestly, her dad was muscular, which scared the living shit out of me. When I get to the basement, he tells me to take a seat on a love seat across from his chair.

"Sir, I really can just go, I don't want to be somewhere where I'm unwanted."

"Dominic, it's okay. You can stay here for as long as you want. Christine, her mom, is the one that has a problem with it. But the last time I checked I paid for this whole damn house."

I sit there in silence not knowing what to say. He reaches into his pocket and pulls out chewing tobacco.

"You want some?" He asks.

"Oh no, I don't use any form of tobacco."

"Good for you. I have only one rule that you have to follow."

"What's that sir?"

"Well actually two rules, don't call me sir, call me Jeff. But the main rule is, be there for Alyssa no matter what. Losing Bryan has been hard on all of us. You're a respectful kid so I expect that rule won't be problem."

"It won't," I say.

"I think Alyssa is waiting for you, she's in her room. Christine will get you a mattress to sleep on, in the living room. Although both you and I know that for most of the night you'll be sleeping with Alyssa, don't let Christine catch you. I'll holler at you later though," he says grinning.

"Thank you," I say, shaking his hand.

I walk upstairs, a little confused. Alyssa's dad was just calm with the whole idea of me staying here. He even offered me tobacco. At least I know he doesn't mind me being here, which is very surprising. I pass the kitchen as I walk down the hall to Alyssa's room. I quietly open the door as she's laying down, listening to music.

"Hey," she says with a smile.

I didn't say anything, rather I smile back, while I lay next to her.

"Has anyone told you how beautiful you are?" I say.

"Aw Dom, quit," she says blushing.

"Well I just want you to know, you're the most beautiful girl on earth."

"You're the sweetest guy ever."

I take my arms and wrap them around her. I stare into her eyes as I go in for a kiss. Expecting this moment to be interrupted, our lips finally touch. It is everything I thought it was going to be. From the tingles in my lips to the heat beneath my hands where they grip her waist. After what feels like a lifetime, I pull her on top of me. Gripping her hips tighter, I bring her as close to me as possible, while I slide my hands down her body. I hear a vague knock at the front door, but don't think much about it and continue to kiss her passionately. Moments later, her dad interrupts by walking into her room.

"Dominic, this is for you," he says as I jump.

"Okay?" I say confused.

Her dad hands me the package, then walks out of the room. I carefully rip the package open. Inside there is a rolled-up piece of paper with string tied around it. I untie the paper, curiously as I look at Alyssa. After I untie the paper, I carefully roll out the twelve by nine paper. In the top left-hand corner there is writing that reads, *"Clue One."* My eyes then immediately shoot down to the short writing below.

*"Hello Dominic Wilkerson,*

*Hot Springs, a city that has more secrets than the Central Intelligence Agency. Be careful who you associate with. The ones closest to you can be the enemy. Dominic, you're not the target, you're the key. I've written up seven clues that will start to give you answers to everything the whole world wants to know. With those answers you may choose to keep them to yourself or you may make it headline news. Just understand that you're needed no matter what, so don't live in fear, live in clarity. I chose to be someone that I'm not and for that I have been living in disguise. But now, I leave it up to you to share my true identity, and that you won't figure out until the last clue. Dominic, you can't hide. You're being constantly watched by the enemy and the ally. Just know I'm the ally and I'm working to help you. My sister disappeared when I was just three years old and I went missing when I was six. ~K"*

I sit there for a couple minutes pondering to myself, who is K? I re-read the paper and that's when an idea hit me.

"Do you have a computer?" I ask Alyssa.

She goes to her closet and pulls out a bag. Inside the bag she pulls out her laptop and hands it to me.

"What's going on?" She asks.

Instead of responding, I hand her the paper to read. I quickly open the laptop and type in *"Katherine Dobell."* I click on the memorial page for her.

*"Katherine Marie Dobell was born in Hot Springs, Arkansas on July 7, 1994. Katherine is the daughter of Stan and Kimberly Dobell. Katherine is also the younger sister of the infamous Sidney Dobell. Katherine was a sweet young girl that was taken away too soon at the age of six. Katherine was never found but there were many leads on her whereabouts. Even though Katherine was never found, we know she's in a better place singing with the angels with Sidney."*

I remember hearing this story as a young kid because it was the second biggest mystery in Hot Springs. Authorities also believed that a creep abducted her because they were obsessed with Sidney. Although there were many leads, none of them checked out in the end. Stan and Kimberly Dobell soon moved out of Arkansas and no one has seen them since. I look at Alyssa as if she already knows.

"I'm always going to be right by your side, I promise," Alyssa tells me.

"Thank you," I say as I kiss her.

"I have to go sleep on the air mattress," I say.

"Please stay," she begs.

"I would but I kind of like being here, so I probably should do what your mom wants."

"I like you being here too, but they'll be going to bed soon, so what will they know? If you're on the air mattress by the time they wake up, we'll be fine," she says giving me a flirtatious smile.

"You make a good argument. I guess I could slip into your bed," I say pulling her close to me.

I slide my hands from her waist down to her hip and grip her butt pulling her body so close to me that I can feel her heart speed up. She wraps her arms around my neck pulling me down to kiss her. The kissing becomes more intense with every second that goes by. I start pushing towards the door, hearing a small thud. With her back pressed against the door, I feel her hands slide down my chest to the bottom of my shirt. She rips it off over my head. So many thoughts are running through my mind, but I shove them aside. I grasp the bottom of her oversize t-shirt and slowly pull it over her body, running my hands against her skin. I hear a knock at the door and Alyssa pushes me off, jumping into her bed. I quickly throw my shirt back on. I open the door, but no one is there. I give her a kiss goodnight and head off to the living room.

I find the mattress blown up with blankets all over it in the living room. The living room was dark as I barely could see. I hear a strange noise but decide to not start over thinking. When I get under the blanket and close my eyes, a light flickers on. It's Alyssa's mom on the couch in the corner. I stare at her as my heart begins to beat out of my chest.

"Hey, Mrs. Washburn," I say shaking.

She just stares at me with what feels like beams digging into my skin.

"So Dominic, what are they doing to my son, Bryan?"

"Uh, who are you talking about?"

"Dominic, let's not play dumb here."

"Mrs. Washburn, I need you to explain."

"God dammit you know what the hell I'm talking about! What are they doing to Bryan?" She yells, breaking into tears.

I begin to feel like I'm having a heart attack. The sweat pours down my face as I find myself having a hard time breathing.

"Mom. what's going on?"

I look to my left to see Alyssa. I get up as I rush over to her.

"Dominic, what'd you do to Bryan? Are you a part of the disappearances in Sido? Dominic, did you hurt my brother?"

"No!" I plea.

64

"Are you lying to me? Do you know what I do to the people that hurt those close to me and lie?"

All the sudden I feel a jab into my stomach. I look down, to find a knife cut into my abdominal area. Alyssa pulls out the knife and jabs it back in, laughing as she continues. I begin to cry as I feel betrayed by someone I trusted. When she goes to stab for a third time my eyes shoot open, my whole body is drenched in sweat. I look around the room, slowly. When I see the clock, I realize I've only been asleep for a couple hours. I decide to get up and change out of my soaked clothes. Once I change, I lay back down to only find myself still awake an hour later. I get back up and walk down the hallway to Alyssa's room. She is rolled on her side, when I lay beside her I wrap my arms around her.

"Hey," she says smiling. "What's wrong?"

"Bad dream."

"Aw babe, just stay in here from now on," she says, grabbing my hand tightly.

"I will," I say falling asleep.

∞ ∞ ∞

The morning sunshine glares on my face as I wake up. I notice something different, Alyssa is no longer in the bed with me. I can hear voices coming from the living room area. I get up very quietly and open the door. I sneak into the kitchen without anyone

65

noticing so I can listen to their conversation. I stand there motionless, scared to even breathe because they may hear me.

"Remember, don't let your feelings get in your way, there's one mission so stick to it," says Mr. Washburn.

"We're a family, I love you both," says Mrs. Washburn.

"May I be dismissed?" I hear Alyssa ask.

"Alyssa, we're serious."

"I know Dad."

Quickly, I grab a cup to act like I'm getting a glass of water. While I'm filling the cup up, I feel a presence surround me.

"Good morning, son," says Mr. Washburn.

"Good morning, Mr. Washburn," I say with a blank stare.

"Remember, you can just call me Jeff."

"Yes sir, I mean Jeff."

I turn around to Alyssa standing there.

"Let's go to my room," Alyssa says laughing.

I follow her and lay next to her. I grab her, bringing her close to me to the point where are bodies are intertwined. So many emotions are running through my mind. At first her and I sit there without speaking a word, but after several minutes she breaks the silence.

"What's wrong babe?"

"Just the dream I had, it felt so real."

"Do you want to talk about it?" She asks.

"Yeah. Your mom started screaming at me, accusing me of your brother's disappearance. Then you came out accusing me of lying and started stabbing me."

She begins to laugh, as if it was funny.

"I'm sorry," she says laughing. "But why do you think you dreamed that?"

"I don't know, I think it's the fear of losing you."

"Dom, I know I've said this, but I promise I'm not leaving your side, and don't fear losing me because I'm not going to let that happen. If something does happen, it wouldn't be me, it would be my parents."

"I hope you keep that promise, because I've never met someone so special like you."

She just smiles and looks at me before going in for a kiss. A kiss that held a promise, but before it could continue any further, Alyssa's mom interrupts.

"Hey Dominic, come out here there's something you might want to see."

I grab Alyssa's hand as we walk into the living room where there is breaking news on the television.

"Breaking news, the administrator that was connected with the disappearance of Bryan Washburn and injured Dominic Wilkerson has been identified as Principal Roger Hawkins. It was also discovered that Principal Hawkins is the uncle of deceased

Assistant Principal, Dr. Mary Nunez. Investigators believe he has no connection to her death," says the news reporter.

If nothing could get any stranger, it has. Never in a million years did I see Principal Hawkins being Dr. Nunez's uncle. I sat there in utter silence, knowing that Principal Hawkins had nothing to do with what happened. Had Principal Hawkins not covered up for Dr. Nunez, then she may still be alive. Although, if she would've got locked up, I would've never seen the camera footage or got to read the letter from my dad.

"Hey, how about we go get some breakfast, what do you say?" Mr. Washburn asks breaking up the silence.

"Sweetie, I look like a hot mess," says Mrs. Washburn.

"Well, go get ready then, what are you waiting for?"

After about forty-five minutes of Mrs. Washburn and Alyssa getting ready, we finally head to Megan's Diner. Alyssa and I sit in the back seats, with her head resting on my chest during the car ride. Once we arrive at Megan's Diner, we are immediately seated, which is quite unusual. I order what I always get, the Ultimate Omelette, the best omelette around. While I wait for the omelette, I look up at the TV and freeze. I tap Alyssa on her shoulder as her eyes also shoot towards the TV.

"More breaking news out of Hot Springs. Seventeen-year-old Dominic Wilkerson has went missing. His mother says she hasn't seen him since sometime last night. If you have any tips of his whereabouts please call the hotline below," says a news lady.

"Should we take you back home?" Alyssa asks.

"Hell no, I'm never going back. All she did was lie to me."

"Dom, that's your mom. I'm sure she loves and cares about you."

"Yeah, I'm sure she does."

I get up, furious, and leave the restaurant. I sit on the bench just outside of Megan's Diner. A couple minutes later, Alyssa comes out and sits next to me. She puts her head against my shoulder.

"Your food is at the table," she says.

"I don't want it."

"Dom, I'm sorry. I don't want you to go back home because I love being with you. I was just saying I'm sure she never meant to hurt you."

"Yeah, well I always get hurt. I'm sure you'll hurt me in the end too, like everyone else."

"Babe stop! For the trillionth time, I'm not going to hurt you!"

I get up and walk back into Megan's Diner. My omelette sitting there sizzling hot, I ask the waiter for a to go box.

"Do we need to take you back home?" Mr. Washburn asks.

"No, it's fine, as long as it's fine with you."

"Yes, of course. All we'd like for you to do is let your mom know you're okay. If you want to tell her where you are that's completely up to you, but we don't mind having to talk to her if needed."

"I will and thank you guys for letting me stay with you, it means a lot."

"No problem, son," says Mr. Washburn.

The waiter comes back with a to go box for my omelette. I stuff the omelette into my to go box while I wait for everyone else to finish eating. I sit there, just staring at the table, my stomach begins to grumble. Once the ticket is paid, I get up. Alyssa grabs my hand as we walk out the doors and to the car. While we near Alyssa's house, Mrs. Washburn begins to talk to me.

"So Dominic, may I speak to you in private when we get to the house?"

"Yes, of course Mrs. Washburn."

"Good," she says with a smirk.

Alyssa could tell I was getting nervous about talking to her mom, so she started rubbing my arm, trying to calm me down. When we get back to the house, Alyssa goes to her room and Mr. Washburn goes to his man cave. I follow Mrs. Washburn into the living room and sit next to her on the couch.

"I like you Dominic, and that's hard to come by. You seem like a good kid that wants nothing but peace."

"Yes ma'am, I don't like conflict."

"Well good, I wish other people's minds were like yours, but sadly there's a world of conflict."

"Yes there is, but with all due respect what does this have to do with me?"

She smiles, "Very soon you'll have the choice of what you want. Just stick to wanting no conflict and everything in life will run smoothly."

"Okay? May I go be with Alyssa now," I say feeling a sense of confusion.

"Yes, you may, and from now on you can sleep back there with Alyssa."

When I begin to walk away, Mrs. Washburn says, "Hey Dom, no one needs to know we had this conversation, okay?"

I nod my head and walk back to Alyssa's room. I'm confused, why would it be okay now? I really didn't understand or know what to think.

"What'd my mom want?"

"She was just talking about me treating you right and taking care of you."

"See, it wasn't so bad, was it?"

"No, she also told me from now on I can sleep back here with you with her permission!"

"Really? That's great! It was lonely last night until you snuck back into my room."

"Well now you don't have to feel like that again because from now on I'll have you in my arms."

71

I look at her and can do nothing but smile. She rubs her hands against my chest with a frown.

"What's wrong?" I ask

"I'm having a lot of regret."

"Over what?"

"Nothing. It doesn't matter."

"Babe, it matters."

"Dom, let me ask you something."

"Yes?"

"What's your biggest fear?"

"You already know, it's losing you."

"Besides that."

"Literally my biggest fear is losing you."

"You don't need to worry about that though."

"Well I'm prepared to have my heart broken again."

"Again?"

"Yes, everything that comes into my life, leaves."

Before she can continue the conversation, her mom calls us in for dinner. I grab Alyssa's hand and we walk into the kitchen.

"Grab as much food as you desire, there's plenty," says Mrs. Washburn.

I grab a little bit of everything, then I sit next to Alyssa. I eat slowly, trying not to portray myself as a pig. While we're eating, Mrs. Washburn's phone begins to ring.

"Hello?" Mrs. Washburn answers.

Her face goes from confusion to pale in a matter of seconds. She just sits there, listening, with tears rushing down her face. Then three words flutter out of her mouth and asks, "So he's alive?"

# CHAPTER SIX

When Mrs. Washburn hangs up the phone she goes into a complete meltdown. Alyssa and I sit there clueless, not knowing what Mrs. Washburn was told. Mr. Washburn rushes over to Mrs. Washburn and corrals her into his arms.

"What's wrong, baby?"

"Bryan was found and taken to St. Vincent hospital."

When Mrs. Washburn says this my stomach immediately drops. I look over at Alyssa to see tears begin rolling down her face. Mr. Washburn sits there with his jaw dropped, practically emotionless. After a few minutes of silence, Mr. Washburn grabs the car keys.

"What are we waiting for? Let's go see Bryan!"

I grab Alyssa's hand as we head outside to the car. I don't even know what to think anymore, with the death of Dr. Nunez, Dr. Hawkins being her uncle, and the conversation about conflict earlier today. The last few days have made Hot Springs an even bigger mystery, that's starting to haunt me. I open the car door for Alyssa, and when she gets in I close it for her. Once I get in the car I look at her and grab her hand.

"Thank you so much for being so caring," she says.

"Of course, I always will be here for you."

Alyssa just smiles as she lays her head on my lap. I begin to run my fingers through her hair as I try to figure out why everything is happening. I remember that I need to contact my mom about me being okay. I reach in my pocket to pull out my phone. Initially, I was going to call her, but I don't feel like talking to her, so I just text her that I'm okay. I lay my head against the window as I just blankly stare at the stars. Several minutes later, we arrive at St. Vincent's. I step out of the car and take a deep breath. I catch myself just staring at the structure of the hospital realizing I was here not too long ago. Alyssa comes up beside me, holding onto my arm. Alyssa and I follow her parents into the hospital, where we head to the trauma unit. Mr. Washburn checks in at the desk and almost immediately we all are taken to Bryan's room. The nurse directs us to his room and then looks at me with a weird gaze.

"Be careful," the nurse whispers as she walks past me.

All these warnings directed towards me, but for what? Is everyone watching me? Is this the Truman show? All this confusion is leaving me in fear of the unknown. Alyssa and I walk into the room where Bryans near lifeless body lies. I take a seat in a chair as the Washburns and Alyssa grab Bryan's hand. Bryan's nurse comes in and explains how he got to St. Vincents.

"Nice to meet you Mr. and Mrs. Washburn," says the nurse, shaking their hands.

"Nice to meet you, too."

"About an hour ago Bryan was found by a local on McLeod street just lying on the side of the road. How he got there? No one knows. A local immediately called 911, but by the time emergency personnel arrived the local was no longer there. The ambulance was here in no time and once stabilized we called you guys. I just want to give you fair warning that the media will be here in no time to cover the story of your son being found. Since being here, he has been unresponsive, but we expect him to become responsive in the coming days. All that matters is that he's going to make it and tests are being ran right now."

"Are the law enforcement going to try to investigate to whom the local was?" Mrs. Washburn asks.

"I'm sorry, Mrs. Washburn, but I can't answer that due to my lack of knowledge on the case. All I know is he's in great care. Mr. Washburn, can I talk with you outside the room really quick?"

"Of course."

The nurse and Mr. Washburn step outside of the room as I sit there with Alyssa doing my best to comfort her. The room is as silent as a library and all I can do is think about everything that's happened since the last day of school. Lives have been lost, people have been injured, and most of all some relationships have become stronger as others have dissipated. A rush of fear hits me. What if things just get worse? Who else will die? Who else will be hurt whether, that's emotional or physical? At the end of this, if there is an end, will Alyssa still be by my side? All I have ever been thinking about are things I can't control. I pull my phone out to check the time and see that my mom has responded to my text.

"Dominic Allen Wilkerson! Come home now! I've been worried sick about you," my mom responded.

I just swipe over on the text like it never existed. After a while Mr. Washburn finally comes back in the room.

"Hey honey, are you ready to go home?"

"That's fine."

I get up as Alyssa and I quickly walk out of Bryan's room. Once we are about halfway to the car, the Washburns stop and tell us they need to go do something and toss me their car keys. A couple minutes later Alyssa and I arrive at the car as we hop in the back seats.

"Dom," Alyssa says quietly.

"Yes?"

"I'm sorry I've been so reserved tonight, my mind is just going crazy," she says.

"It's okay, babe, I understand."

"Okay good," she says with a smile.

I smile and give her a kiss as she lays her head on me. It felt like she wanted to say something else but was hesitant to do so. Her and I just lie there waiting on her parents. A couple minutes later her parents get in the car and we head on home. The whole ride back to her house I imagine what it would be like if none of us would've went to Sido that gut-wrenching night. But has Sido broken its own rules because Bryan and I have been taken to the hospital with the help of someone within Sido. The more and more I think about it, the more my head feels like it's going to explode. Maybe I should go back home and give my mom another chance. Then again, I feel like after what happened I don't know her. Now I've invested all my trust into Alyssa, just praying that she doesn't do anything to compromise that trust.

After a thoughtful car ride home, I give Alyssa a piggy back ride all the way to her room. I gently lay her onto her bed as she pulls me down on top of her. From there, her and I kiss for several moments. She then grabs my hand and gently rubs my fingers.

"Dom, there was something else I wanted to tell you earlier," she says.

"What's that?" I ask, a little worried.

"When I'm with you I get this feeling that I've never felt before."

"Aw me too," I say relieved.

"But that feeling makes me not just like you... Dom, I'm falling in love with you," she says with a slight blush.

I can't help but smile. I feel a million butterflies dancing within myself. I never thought I would ever hear Alyssa say that to me.

"Alyssa," I say with a pause. "I'm falling in love with you too."

Again, her and I just begin to kiss until we both start to feel tired. Before we fall asleep, I roll over to her side, wrap my arms around her and fall sound asleep.

∞ ∞ ∞

The night was a restless one. I figured since Alyssa was beside me I'd sleep better, but instead I had a rude awakening when all I could do is stare at the ceiling. Quietly, I get up and start toward the kitchen where I can hear the Washburns. They speak to each other as if everything is classified information and if what they say is compromised the whole world will come to an end. I purposely kick the wall, so they'll hear me coming out, therefore, it's not awkward when I interrupt their conversation. I take a seat on the couch that faces their sixty-inch flat screen TV. Of course, the news is on and I see the house I'm sitting in on TV. The story is captioned, "Bryan Washburn is Alive." I get up and peek out the window. Immediately I'm in awe of what I see. The entire street is filled with what looks like close to a hundred-different news stations from what appears to be from multiple states. I throw myself back and continue watching the news broadcast. Mr. Washburn walks out of the kitchen into the living room and just stares at the TV.

"Crazy, huh? We're the biggest news story in the nation right now," Mr. Washburn says staring at the TV.

"Yeah, it is," I say.

"What's even crazier is these stupid reporters keep talking about how Christine and I don't care about our son since we're just lying around at home right now. Those dumbass people don't even know how it feels to be in our situation."

"Yeah it's messed up."

"You're right. I've tried being the best damn father I could be and now I'm getting publicly shamed by the media, and oh my son might not even remember who I am when he wakes up."

"I'm sorry, Jeff."

"You should be, it's all your damn fault," he says, walking back into the kitchen.

All my fault? I think. It's not my fault? It's Dr. Nunez's fault because this was her grand idea. Part of me wants to go off on Mr. Washburn but another part won't let me for Alyssa's sake. I just quietly lie there until Alyssa comes out and lays next to me.

"Good Morning baby," I say.

"Good Morning," she says, kissing me.

"How'd you sleep?" I ask.

"Great, what about you?"

"Not so great."

"Why's that?"

"I don't know, just couldn't stop thinking."

"Hmm, maybe tonight I can make you stop thinking for a little bit," she says biting her lower lip.

Smirking back at her I pull her hard against me.

"Trust me, the only thing that will be going to through my mind tonight is you."

Her and I continue to hangout in the living room, while we watch the news. Alyssa cuddles up next to me and I wrap my arms around her.

"Tonight, the city of Hot Springs will hold a vigil for their beloved Assistant Principal, Dr. Nunez. The vigil will be held at the high school at seven o'clock. She died at the age of twenty-eight and will be dearly missed," says the news lady.

She died way too young but maybe it was karma that came back around and sadly took her life. If only I could have one last conversation with her to ask her every question I have at this point. Just as I become more comfortable on the couch, the doorbell rings.

"I'll get it," Alyssa yells.

When Alyssa comes back up the stairs, she is carrying a similar package that I got the other night. My heart begins to pound as I know it's probably another clue.

"I think this is for you," Alyssa says, handing me the package.

I quickly open it, seeing there is another folded piece of paper. I unravel the paper to see *"Clue two"* in the top left-hand corner. I lower my eyes where there is more writing.

*"Guessing you figured out that I'm Katherine Dobell. I don't want you to tell. Dominic, you're a bright person with an even brighter future. When one major event is discovered you will discover a new clue. The girl that lies next to you is a cute one but be careful. Does she really want you? Do what your heart tells you to do, not your head. The Washburns are shady people, I know their true identity, but I won't spoil that just yet as I know you'll figure it out yourself. Also, it was brave of you to knock some sense into Bryan on the last day of school."* -K

I look at Alyssa but when I look at her all I want to believe is she's the one. I tell myself I'm not going to let someone I don't even know destroy our relationship. I didn't sign up for these subscriptions of clues. With my fingers I crumble the clue into a ball and slide it into my pocket.

"What did it say?" Alyssa asks.

"Nothing that matters."

"Babe, tell me."

"Let's go take a walk."

Alyssa and I get off the couch and head out the door. Immediately we are overcome by the media. Her and I walk down her street away from the media before I say anything. As I'm about to say something I realize I shouldn't because she's reassured me a million times she'd never hurt me.

"That paper was clue two, here read it for yourself," I say, handing her the crumbled paper.

She reads the paper, then hands it back to me. She just keeps walking, but with her head down. I see a tear shed down her face. Quickly, I stop and put my arms around her.

"I would never intentionally hurt you," she says softly.

"Are you going to hurt me?"

"I don't plan on it, but how does she know about the fight on the last day of school?"

I remember reading that part but everything else she said got to me, so I forgot all about the fight.

"I don't know, maybe word of mouth?"

"There's no way it would have got to her, she purposely put that in there. These are clues not just random statements."

Holy shit, she's right. I don't pay attention to the actual clues. It's like Katherine is a ghost that knows everything that happens to me. Now everywhere I go I feel like someone is watching me.

"Alyssa, I don't know what to do anymore. My mind is constantly racing about every damn scenario that could happen."

"That's why I'm here, so we can get through it together."

"But people aren't targeting you! I'm some centerpiece that I have no idea to what's even going on."

"Just give it some more time, then it'll all make sense. I promise."

Alyssa and I continue walking around the neighborhood. Not much was said for the rest of the walk. Whatever is happening in Hot Springs, I hope it ends soon because it's killing me inside. It isn't hard to figure out the Washburns are shady, but I don't feel in any danger while staying with them. Alyssa and I walk past the school where the vigil for Dr. Nunez will be held. The same school where Dr. Nunez and I had a conversation about going to Sido. It's where it all started and soon it must come to an end.

"Let's go back home, watch movies, eat dinner, then go to the vigil," I say.

Alyssa nods as we start back to her house. The media has cleared up some, so it wasn't so crowded around her house. When her and I get inside we cuddle and watch movies all day. It was a perfect imperfect day that I wouldn't have traded for the world. It consisted of laughter, cute conversations, and most of all, happiness. The Washburns left us with dinner before they went to St. Vincent's to see Bryan. After a day spent with her, my mind feels cleared for the first time in a while. Her and I go and eat dinner, then get dressed.

It only took me half an hour to get ready, so I sit and wait for Alyssa to finish getting ready. When she comes out she looks so amazing in a light green summer floral dress and my breath is taken away.

"Wow, you look beautiful," I say.

"Aw, you look very handsome yourself."

"Ready?" I ask.

"Yes."

Emotion overcomes my body, while Alyssa and I walk to the school. The person that has caused me so many problems, is actually gone. Only I wish she was still here, she was my answer to everything. There are many people gathered on the football field, where the field lights make it feel like day. Several news trucks surround the school as they're probably hoping to find me or Alyssa. I stand near the back of the vigil as people start turning heads, looking at me. Candles are lit all over the place. Someone I didn't know comes up to Alyssa and I, handing us a lit candle.

It's full of raw emotion that I can't describe. I stand there wondering if I could've prevented her death. Suddenly, I feel something touch me, I look back to see a black figure running back into the parking lot. I dart for the parking lot keeping the figure in my sight. Finally, I see them go into the Kidz Country parking lot. I follow as the figure jumps out at me. I'm stunned to see who it is and my body goes into shock.

"Dr. Hawkins, how did you get out of jail?"

"Shh, I'm here to help you."

"What do you want?"

"Dr. Nunez wanted me to watch out for you in case something happened to her. I'm going into hiding but still watching out for you, I have the answers to your questions."

In that moment a sense of sincerity hit me, I may just get my questions answered finally.

"Meet me at the cemetery tomorrow morning before the crack of dawn," Dr. Hawkins says. "Also, you need to stay away from the Washburns, they're not good people."

More questions rise as Dr. Hawkins disappears, what seems like to be out of thin air. Alyssa comes running, asking me questions, but her voice becomes background noise as I begin to walk home, and what I mean by home is my actual home.

# CHAPTER SEVEN

Step by step, I near the house that I promised myself I would never go back to. Alyssa is following me, yet for some reason I pretend like she doesn't exist. My heart is crushing inside but in this moment, I'm thinking with my head. Eventually I turn around and say something I'll later regret.

"What's your problem? Do you not get it? I don't want to be around you. Go home and stop talking to me," I say, not realizing what came out of my mouth.

The look on her face, I can tell how hurt she is. When I see the beautiful girl I love, hurt because of something I said, I almost break down. I couldn't look at her anymore, so I just turn away and head towards my house crying. I hurt her so bad, I was in such disgust with myself. After five minutes of walking home, I change my direction back to where I left her all by herself. What if something bad happens to her now? I feel so stupid. My walking turns into a sprint. When I get to where I left her, she is no longer there. Her house isn't too far away so I run to her house. I knock on her door and I'm greeted by Mr. Washburn.

"Hey Dom, where's Alyssa?"

I don't even respond and jet away from her house on a search to find her. My stomach begins to become uneasy not knowing her safety. I go all over the place to find her, but an hour later there's still no sign of her. I think long and hard on where she could be. Then it hit me, "The River." I dead sprint because I know I need to find her soon. When I arrive at the river I see Alyssa just staring at the ripples in the water. Quietly, I near her and take a seat next to her. Motionless, she continues to look at the river as if I'm nonexistent.

"Babe..."

"Don't call me that," she responds.

"I'm sorry, please forgive me."

"Forgive you? You hurt my feelings, I thought you were different. I didn't think you were a douchebag like every other guy out there, but guess what, you are. I thought you cared about me."

"No, I promise I'm not, I got overwhelmed with everything going on."

"Clearly you are, so stop making promises that aren't true."

"Alyssa please, you mean the world to me. I love who you are, I love what we're becoming, and most of all I love you," I say in a cracky voice.

"Do you mean that?"

"Of course I do, I can't imagine my life without you."

"Even though you're a jerk, I love you too," she says.

I grab her hand and together we walk back to her house. When Alyssa and I get home, I couldn't help but think about how beautiful Alyssa is. With a small smile on my face, I grab her hand and lead her towards her bed. Her and I sit down, where I turn to face her, staring deeply into her gorgeous blue eyes.

"Alyssa, you know I love you. I wouldn't do anything to hurt you on purpose. You're the best thing that has happened to me and I'd never do anything to lose you."

She looks up at me with the biggest smile on her face as her eyes are sparkling with amusement.

"I know," she says as she leans towards me, wrapping her arms around my neck, pulling me closer to her, so I grab her hips and pull her on top of me, while her legs are straddling my hips.

She deepens the kiss, gripping my shirt tight in her hand. I clutch onto her hips, sliding my hands beneath her shirt. Her skin felt hot beneath my fingers. I couldn't help but wonder how I managed to find a girl like her. Almost as if she was reading my mind she sits up and looks down at me.

"I know you may think I'm the best thing that has happened to you, but I want you to know while that may be true for you, it isn't true for me."

At first, I didn't understand her. With confusion written in my face she swings her leg back over me and turns her body sideways, so she faces me.

"I'm not saying you're not the best thing that has happened to me because you're not, you're more than that. I never thought I would fall so hard for someone until I met you and the craziest thing is that it all happened slowly until all the sudden it hit me all at once. Which by far is the best feeling in the world."

I knew in this moment Alyssa and I have connected on a much deeper level. I pull her close to me, feeling her snuggle against me. I wrap my arms around her, holding her tight. It was like we would never let each other go, which is a perfect ending to a crappy day. But I know tomorrow will be a day I can't prepare for.

∞ ∞ ∞

I hear the sounds of nature as I wake up. I look to my right, just to find Alyssa no longer beside me. I lay in bed for a couple of moments trying to clear my mind. I look at my phone to see it's already seven. I get up and throw some different clothes on because I realize I have to meet Dr. Hawkins at the cemetery. When I walk into the hall I can hear commotion in the kitchen. I peek my head around the corner to find Alyssa and her parents talking. I quietly begin down the stairs but before I can get to the door I hear Alyssa clear her throat.

"Where are you going?"

"Just for a walk."

"Want me to come?"

"No, I want to be alone."

"Okay be careful."

I continue back down the stairs and out the door. I take a deep breath after I close the door behind me. As much as I would love for her to come, it probably wouldn't be wise. I begin to do a light jog, so I can get to the cemetery faster. After about fifteen minutes I arrive at Greenwood Cemetery. I walk around for five minutes until I spot Hawkins near the tree line. I slowly walk to where he is standing.

"You're a little late," he says, smiling, looking at his watch.

"Yeah, sorry."

"Let's take a walk around and talk," he says.

Hawkins and I walk for minutes before either one of us says anything.

"So, why are the Washburns not good people?" I ask.

"Let's just say they were against your father and hell I'm pretty sure Nunez was killed by them."

I'm startled but I try to stay calm, so I can get as many answers as possible.

"My mom, is she a good person?"

"Yes Dominic, she is. She told me what happened between the two of you. You should go see her."

"You spoke to her?"

"Yes. Your dad and I were close, so I check in on your mom's well-being occasionally."

I wanted to ask him how he escaped jail but at this point that answer doesn't really matter. I try to think hard of what else I want to ask.

"Do you know what Sido really is?"

"I can't discuss that with you."

"Why? Don't I have the right to know?"

"Time will give you answers but before I let you loose on your way home I want to give you some advice. Don't trust anyone especially that girlfriend of yours, but don't question her or her family because they're vicious people so just stay to what you're doing. Also, one last thing, don't go to the police for anything because they're not good people either. Just go back to what happened in 1976, they don't even care if you're one of their own."

Dr. Hawkins turns around and disappears into the trees. I stand there in silence, alone in the cemetery. I turn back to the entrance, so I can head back to the Washburns. The walk back was one of those walks where you don't remember walking at all because of the thoughts running through your head. Dr. Hawkins may have given me answers to some of my questions, but new questions have hit me. I understand not everything will be answered, but all I want is to be less confused. When I arrive back at the Washburns, Alyssa is outside waiting on me. I walk up to her and give her a kiss.

"Would you mind going to the hospital with me to see Bryan?" She asks.

"Of course not."

Her and I walk into the house as her parents are walking down the stairs.

"Is Dominic going to go to the hospital, too?" The Washburns ask Alyssa.

"Yes, he is."

"If you insist," says Mrs. Washburn.

Alyssa and I get in the back of the Suburban. The ride to the hospital felt intense although no one said a word. It was like I did something wrong that I didn't know about. Once we arrive at the hospital, the Washburns lead the way to where Bryan's nearly lifeless body lies. As soon as the door to Bryan's room shuts behind me, Bryan opens his eyes for the first time since that night in Sido. He turns his head to where I stand and stares at me.

"Him!" Bryan says, pointing at me.

"What?" Mr. Washburn asks.

"He's my best friend," Bryan says with a smile.

My eyes shoot open as I'm caught by total shock. Bryan Washburn just called me his best friend. The same Bryan Washburn that tried to fight me. Clearly, he isn't in the right state of mind and probably doesn't even know who I am.

"Dominic Wilkerson, the kid who saved me from those people trying to hurt me," Bryan says out loud.

"Wait, what?" Alyssa says as her eyes shoot like lasers into mine.

"I promise I didn't help him, I thought he was dead."

"Dominic, you did help me. You told me that you were saving me from my parents," he says.

"Bryan, your parents are right next to you."

"My parents are dead, what are you talking about?" Bryan responds.

Chills rush down my body as I can see Mr. and Mrs. Washburns faces. I run out of the room trying to wake up from this dream, but I know this isn't a dream. I run into the bathroom and throw water all over my face. After about ten minutes, I walk back into the room where Alyssa and her parents are sobbing. I walk over to the Washburns to offer any comfort I can.

"Mrs. Washburn, this same thing happened to me when I first woke up in the hospital. It's whatever drugs they gave us that makes us forget the past. They also held him captive longer, so they may have brainwashed him into believing you both were dead."

"Dominic, the thing is that, we aren't his parents. He's our nephew," says Mrs. Washburn.

∞ ∞ ∞

I believe in this moment; my mind is officially blown. Literal shock is felt throughout my whole body. I get up and walk out of the room and take a seat in the lobby. Dr. Hawkins is right. I

94

don't know these people at all. Who knows at this point if they are even a real family. Out of my peripherals I see Mr. Washburn come over and take a seat next to me.

"Look, Dominic. We're all sorry that we didn't tell you sooner. Christine and I adopted Bryan and Alyssa after their parents were killed when they were little. Their parents weren't good people," says Mr. Washburn.

"Yeah, apparently neither are you," I say.

"You don't have to like Christine or myself but stay with us for Alyssa's sake. Hell, we won't even bother you two."

"Okay, you ignorant," but I stop myself from finishing the sentence because I see Alyssa come out of the room."

I walk over to Alyssa and grab her hand. Her and I continue to walk to the car that brought me the truth. Her so called parents follow behind us. About mid-way to the car I stop and turn around. Running quickly, I go back to Bryan's room where it seems like he is awaiting my presence.

"Run, run fast and don't look back they are using you," Bryan whispers.

I grab his hand apologizing for the past that he may or may not remember. I walk back to where I had stopped to go back to Bryan's room. I'm startled to see the Washburns and Alyssa still waiting for me.

"Sorry, I forgot my phone in the lobby," I say.

Again, I grab Alyssa's hand and her and I walk to the car. My heart is broken, seeing Bryan in such bad shape. Second by second he is continuing to lose oxygen. A kid that I once hated. He went through so much as a child and now his aunt and uncle are using their niece and nephew for what seems like a bigger plot. I feel like Alyssa truly does love me, but I know when the day comes to betray me she'll have no other choice. That's why I must come up with a plan to ensure the future of my safety.

When we arrive back at her house, I text my mom asking her if she'd like to meet for lunch in about an hour or so. She responds in a blink of an eye saying she is exhilarated with this idea. After I get inside, I go to the room and change my clothes. Alyssa walks in and lies down on the bed.

"I'm going to go have lunch with my mom," I say.

"Do you want me to go?"

"I rather you stay here, just in case she goes rogue."

"Okay. I'm sorry I didn't tell you the truth."

"It's okay, I'm used to being lied to."

"Dom, stop."

I walk out of her room down the stairs where I open the front door and step outside. I still have fifty minutes until my mom and I are supposed to meet so I walk in no hurry. My mom and I decided on meeting at Higdon Square Cafe. It's a bittersweet feeling knowing everything in this city is beginning to unravel. I never could've dreamed I would be in this situation. I continue to walk around the city until I get a text from my mom saying, "I'm here." I happen to only be down the street from the cafe. When I walk into the cafe I spot my mom in a booth right away. I take a seat across from her as she smiles.

"What made you want to see me?" She asks.

"I want your help."

She laughs, "You want my help?"

"Yes. I want to get a group of people together and go back to Sido."

"Honey, that's not a good idea."

"I want you to go with me."

"Absolutely not."

"Mom," she stops me.

"I would but I can't or I risk my own life," she says.

"You haven't changed, everything's always about you," I say.

I get up, "Goodbye," I say. I walk to the front of the door and rush back to Alyssa's. As I'm nearing the house I hear a voice whisper my name. It brought back a feeling of when Dr. Nunez did this exact thing before she died. I look to my right, but no one is there. I continue to walk when a figure walks up beside me, it's Dr. Hawkins.

"You scared me," I say laughing nervously.

"Sorry, I need to talk to you."

Dr. Hawkins finds a curb for us to sit on.

"Listen, I was in the cafe. I've been following you in a sense. I heard your conversation between you and your mom. You cannot go back to Sido, Dominic. It's too dangerous and you being there is just going to stir up unwanted trouble."

"Tell me what's going on in Sido and I won't go."

"I can't tell you and you know that, but let me reiterate. You can't go. Sido isn't what you think it is."

"Well, good talk, Dr. Hawkins, maybe you can say hi when I visit Sido," I say standing up, while I begin to walk back to Alyssa's.

"Dominic don't do it! You'll regret it!" Hawkins yells. I just ignore him and the next thing I know I'm walking into the front door. I walk back to Alyssa's room to find her crying.

"Babe, what's wrong?" I ask.

"You hate me, I've messed everything up."

"No, you haven't. I've just been upset with everything going on lately."

"This came while you were gone," she says handing me an envelope.

I grab the back of the envelope reading, *"Clue Three."* Instantly, a sharp pain shoots across my stomach. I open the envelope to find a piece of paper that is folded. Once I unfold the paper I hesitantly begin to read the clue.

*"Dominic,*

*I hope at this point Dr. Hawkins is taking care of you as he promised. He is truly the last person in this city on your side. At this point I'm sure you want to give Sido another attempt. I'm not opposed to this idea, but you'll need a precisely detailed plan. In this city, you're immortal to others because of your father. You and I have met before, but you probably didn't realize it. You're a smart kid that'll make the right decision in the end. I'm sorry I'll never get to formally introduce myself to you. With whatever you do, watch your back for the other side."*

-Katherine Dobell

Tears rush down my face. This is the saddest thing I've ever read. Although it was sad, I don't understand what the clue is. I've met a lot of people throughout my life, so if I met her five years ago I wouldn't remember. But I guess if I'm immortal I should go ahead and visit Sido again. This time, instead of getting a team together, I'm going to only take Alyssa, if she wants too, that is. She quietly reads the letter.

"You want to go back? She asks."

"Yes."

"Can I go with you?"

"That was the plan, just you and I. They won't hurt me, meaning they won't hurt you, knowing I care about you."

"Let's make this plan," she says.

Her and I agree on going the same way her and I went with Nunez. I explain the whole Hawkins situation with her and how he

99

doesn't want me to go back. It also hit me that Hawkins might have extra defense set up knowing I plan on going back. I give him that, he seems to really care about my well-being. After hours of planning, her and I finally have a plan set in stone. Alyssa and I are both are hungry, so we walk to Sonic to get a bite to eat. The cool breeze sweeps across my face, bringing a smile, knowing how blessed I am to have Alyssa. On our way back home, her and I stop by the park where we swing as the moonlight glistens across her beautiful face. I jump off the swing and throw Alyssa over my shoulders, walking home.

When her and I get to her room, I gently throw her onto her bed. I start kissing her neck, but she stops me.

"Dom, not tonight," she says.

I throw myself off her and she grabs my hand.

"Sorry. Maybe tomorrow," she says.

"It's okay, don't be sorry. I'm just happy to have you beside me right now."

"Good."

Shortly after, her and I fall asleep until a strange noise wakes me up from a nightmare. A whisper that sounds like Bryan's voice says, "Run." I know there is no possible way he is in this room. Then it hit me, but I don't want to believe it. I lie there thinking, how will this all end? How many more lives will be lost? Because I have a feeling Bryan just lost his.

# CHAPTER EIGHT

Life, what is life? For an average person life is living day to day. Whether that's working, building a family, or going to school, it's their way of life. For me, life is different. It becomes more complex when you're the centerpiece of something that you don't know anything about. But while I'm trying to figure out this mystery, people are dying. So, I have to sit here and question myself over each life that is lost. Is it my fault? Could I have prevented it? Did Bryan know he was dying? The average person doesn't have to go over these questions, but then again, I'm not average.

The Washburns got the news this morning that Bryan has passed away. Since then, Alyssa has been an emotional train wreck. The Washburns have been in mourning ever since they got the news of his death. I don't have much emotion towards Bryan's death and I don't understand why it isn't affecting me. All I can do is comfort Alyssa to the best of my ability. Not only did Bryan pass away last night, but Nunez's funeral is today. Dr. Nunez irritated me at times, but now I realize how important she was.

"Do you still want to go to Dr. Nunez's funeral?" I ask Alyssa.

She wipes the tears off her face, "Yeah, let me go take a shower and get ready." I kiss her on the forehead as she goes to get ready. I go through my bag to see what I want to wear but all I have are casual clothes. Without saying anything, I walk about fifteen minutes to a clothes store. Hoping my mom didn't cancel my card, I buy a nice button up shirt and slacks. Luckily, my card is approved and I won't be looking to out of place at Nunez's funeral. The walk home is strange because it feels like people are constantly watching me. Whether or not that's the case I hurry back to Alyssa's. When I get back to Alyssa's, I walk in to find Mr. Washburn waiting for me.

"Can we talk?" He asks.

I follow him downstairs where him and I first had a conversation. Mr. Washburn just looks at me for a second, then takes a seat next to me.

"I know I said I wouldn't bother you, but I want to thank you for being there for Alyssa. Her and Bryan were really close, so I can only imagine how she feels."

"Yeah, I'm doing my best to comfort her."

"Good. Dominic, can I ask you something?"

"Sure."

"What are you most afraid of?"

"Not knowing the truth about my father."

He smiles, "That's your biggest fear?"

"Yes it is, and I'm willing to do whatever it takes to figure out what happened to him."

"I hope you get your answers someday."

At this point, Mr. Washburn is beginning to freak me out, so I stand up and head up the stairs.

"Hey Dominic, how soon do you want these answers?"

I get wide eyed and continue up the stairs into Alyssa's room. My eyes widen again, but for a different reason. Alyssa looks absolutely stunning in a light purple dress that is cut off a couple inches above her knees.

She turns around, "Do you like it?"

Standing there practically speechless, "Uh yes, you look amazing!"

She smiles and continues to get ready. I take my new clothes into the bathroom, so I can get ready. I look at myself in the mirror. I splash water in my face to try to wake me up a little bit. I strip down to my boxers and begin to put my clothes on. After I get done I look at myself in the mirror, shocking myself on how good I look. After several minutes of looking at myself from different angles I walk back into Alyssa's room.

"Damn babe, you really clean up nice," she says.

"Yeah right, look at you."

She smiles, "Are you ready? Uncle Jeff told me I could take his car."

Uncle Jeff, not like that wasn't weird to hear, but at least her and I don't have to walk to the funeral. She gets the keys to the car and her and I head out the door. The funeral is at Patrimony Methodist Church. When Alyssa pulls up to the church, we notice that a lot of people have showed up for Nunez's funeral. I get out of the car and open the door for her, grabbing her hand and walking into the church. For an unknown reason my heart begins to accelerate. I try to take deep breaths but that isn't helping. Alyssa knows I'm feeling anxious and squeezes my hand tighter. My heart slows down when her and I get into the church. There is two women on each side as you walk in handing out pamphlets. I look at the pamphlet, but stop because it starts to bring me to tears. The front of the pamphlet has a picture of Nunez and the day she was born and the day she died. Inside there is a remembrance of Dr. Nunez along with acknowledgements. Then on the back there is a quote that reads,

*"When someone is going through a storm that never ends, you either fight or run. I fought knowing I would lose." ~Dr. Nunez*

A younger guy leads Alyssa and I to our seats that were reserved for us in the front row. I notice when Alyssa and I are walking to our seats, that some people smile at me and others give me weird looks. Alyssa notices my legs shaking so she grabs my hand and holds it tight. On a screen, behind Nunez's closed casket, there are pictures of Nunez throughout her life. The pictures make me teary eyed because she looks so happy. The pastor then comes out to open things up.

"Good afternoon everybody. May I ask that we all bow our heads in prayer."

I bow my head and close my eyes envisioning all my memories of Dr. Nunez.

"Our lord, please help all who are dealing with grief and loss of Mary Nunez. Help them to know that you are the source of all comfort. They may think they will never be whole again, or that they can't survive their pain, but you are a faithful God, whose promises are true. Please remind them that with your help, they will get through all they are facing. May they find your strength in their weaknesses and may your hope and peace fill their hearts. In Jesus' name we ask these things. Amen."

For the remainder of the service, the ones close to Nunez shared memories of her. Some wrote up speeches and others gave impromptu speeches. The last person to give a speech shocked me because it was William, Nunez's brother. The last time I saw him was before we split up into Sido. His speech was very long and heart-warming. He talked about growing up with her and all the memories they shared. By the end of the service my eyes were so dry I couldn't cry anymore. The church was doing a private burial only for close family and friends, which I didn't fall under. Alyssa and I then head to the car, but William stops me before I get to the church entrance.

"Hey, Dominic! It's good to see you again. I'm glad you're okay and got to the hospital safely."

"Thanks, good to see you too," I say wondering if I should pull him aside and ask him whether he gave Alyssa his keys to his truck that night, but I decide not to.

"Sad to not see you at the wake last night," he says.

"I didn't even know there was one. Besides, I had my hands full last night, it would've been hard to make it."

"I see. Well, it was nice seeing you."

"You too."

Alyssa and I walk to the car and head back to her house. Once I'm buckled in I take a deep breath and lay my head against the window. Alyssa reaches over and grabs my hand.

"Babe, calm down, everything will be okay," she says.

I take a deep breath and fall asleep on the way home. When I wake up we're down the street from Alyssa's house. I stretch my body across the seat because my muscles feel tight. When Alyssa and I get back to her house, I immediately take my clothes off and take a shower. After my shower, I lay next to Alyssa, finally calmed down.

"Thanks," I say.

"For what?"

"For being there for me and calming me down."

"Of course, I love you."

"I love you too," I say smiling.

My phone vibrates so I look to see that Dr. Hawkins has texted me saying, "Come outside, need to talk."

"Hey babe, I'm going to go for a walk around the block. I'll be back soon."

"Okay, be careful."

I get up and go outside but I don't see Hawkins. I then get another text saying, "Come down the street a little ways." I walk down the street and eventually I find Hawkins awaiting my presence.

"Look, I know you don't want me to go to Sido, but I have too, for myself," I say.

"I didn't come here to talk you out of going. It's your decision and if something happens, you'll have to deal with the consequences, although I still strongly suggest that you not go."

"Well I'm sorry. I'm going."

"Okay, then. That's your choice. Anyways, I want to give you this envelope. Inside is a letter from Nunez," he says, handing me the envelope.

"Oh, did you just find this?"

"No, I just thought this would be the most appropriate time to give this to you. It's all the answers you want. Hopefully tomorrow you can end this "mystery" once and for all."

My hands begin to shake knowing this is what I have been waiting for. Finally, I'll receive all the answers to my questions, so I'll no longer have to live in confusion.

"Well thanks," I say walking away.

"Dominic. You know you were able to come to the burial, Nunez and I still consider you family."

"I wasn't told so, sorry."

I walk back inside, where I sit on the couch as I'm ready but scared for what is inside. I open it up but then there is a knock at the door. I ignore the knock because I see Mr. Washburn heading to the door. I go back to opening the letter.

"Dominic, it's for you," says Mr. Washburn.

I lay the envelope and letter on the couch and go to the door. A thin man then hands me a package.

"Thank you," I say accepting the package into my hands.

"I need you to sign here for me," says the man.

I quickly sign and rush back inside to find the envelope and letter gone.

∞ ∞ ∞

I go upstairs and lay down on the couch to clear my thoughts where I drift off to sleep. All the sudden, I wake up knowing I can't say anything about the letter being gone because it would cause more bad than good. All I know is, that when I went to the door to accept the package either Christine or Jeff took it. I continue to open the package on the couch and make sure no one is around. After I open the first box there is another box. On the front of the box there is a picture. I flip the picture over to find words saying, *"Uncle Roger Hawkins and Mary 2003."* I glance closer to the picture and that's when I'm hit with a childhood memory.

"Mommy, Mommy."

"What Dominic? I'm trying to have an important conversation with these gentlemen."

"I'm hungry Mommy."

"Honey, give me a couple more minutes."

I went to my room to go play with my toys until she was done with the conversation. At the time I knew it must have been important, but now I understand why.

"Dominic, are you still hungry?"

"Yes, can I have a turkey sandwich cut like triangles?"

"Yes, you can."

"Mommy, who were those guys?"

"They were Daddy's old friends checking up on me."

"What are their names?"

"If I tell you will you stop asking so many questions?"

"Yes!"

"The older man is Roger and the younger man is Scott. Now, here you go, eat your sandwich."

I keep staring at the picture as I remember that day better than I remember yesterday. For about a year after that day, those men would come over on a regular basis, but then as time went on, their appearances decreased. Dr. Hawkins really does look after my mom, and now I see why on the last day of school he didn't give me a harsh punishment. He knew what kind of kid I was and now I'm noticing I've known him all my life. I open the box to find a much smaller box, so I open the small box finding a letter and a diamond wedding band. I open the letter having a good feeling on what it's about.

*"Clue Four*

*Dominic, you're over halfway to the truth but now is when things may begin to get weird. This wedding band is your Grandma's and I know she'll be happy to know that you have it. Whoever you decide one day to marry with this ring, make sure she is the one. I hope that you're doing well, I miss you. I know one day we'll be reunited but that'll be awhile. Keep doing whatever you're doing and never run away, just continue to fight even if you lose."*
*-Katherine Dobell*

I tuck away the ring and letter in my pocket, then I dispose all the boxes into the trash. Alyssa comes out to check on me.

"Is everything okay?" She asks.

"Yeah I was about to come back to your room. I was just trying to clear my thoughts."

"Let's stay out here and watch TV," she says while turning on the TV.

She lays on me and turns it on the news which I haven't watched for a while. Of course, the story they're talking about is Dr. Hawkins escaping from jail.

"Holy shit. Uncle Jeff come here!"

"I'll be damned, I knew that would happen," says Mr. Washburn.

"Wait, what do you mean, Jeff?" I ask.

"Oh nothing. Roger and I have had issues in our past."

I stand up, making my way over to a picture of Mr. Washburn and Dr. Hawkins together. Subsequently, memories come rushing back, every last one as vivid as the day. I laugh and shake my head. I pick up the picture and throw it at Mr. Washburn.

"Dominic, what the hell!" Alyssa yells.

"Do you even know what your uncle's real name is?" I ask Alyssa.

"Yes, why are you being a dumbass?"

"What do you think it is? Jeff?"

"No, it's Mark," she says sarcastically.

"Wow, it's not nice to lie to your niece and nephew like that. Now is it Scott?"

"Dominic, calm down, let's talk," Mr. Washburn says.

"Uncle Jeff, what is he talking about?"

"What the hell is all the noise for?" Mrs. Washburn asks running out of the laundry room.

"It's nothing Christine, just having a little fun," he says.

"Well quiet down, Jesus Christ," she says, going back to doing the laundry.

"Dominic come talk," he says.

"Hell no! Everything you say is bullshit!" I say rushing back to Alyssa's room.

I lie there, curled up in a ball on Alyssa's bed. I can hear Alyssa going off on Mr. Washburn and eventually Christine went out there to settle everything down. About an hour later Alyssa comes in apologizing for everything. More than ever, I'm determined to go to Sido tonight. I hand Alyssa the clue to read but I decide not to tell her about what Dr. Hawkins gave me and how it mysteriously disappeared. After she reads the clue she just gives me this look.

"Dom, I don't understand how these are clues? They sound more like advice to me."

"Yeah, I know, I don't get it, but I guess it's good advice. Do you think that they'll still let you take the car tonight?"

"Oh they will, no question about it."

I smile and Alyssa and I lay down on her bed as she lays her head on my chest and we start watching a movie. I hear a knock at the front door, so I tell Alyssa to be quiet for a second.

"Hi, Mrs. Wilkerson, it's so nice to see you."

Mom? What is she doing here? I think to myself, jumping out of the bed. I rush out there and look her straight into her eyes.

"Hey honey. Can you and I talk?"

I want to shake my head no, but I find myself nodding yes. Her and I talk on the porch so no one else can hear our conversation.

"What do you want?" I ask.

"You remember, don't you?"

"Remember what?"

"When you were six and I made you a sandwich, then told you about those two guys."

"Yeah it came back to me today. Mom, what's going on?"

"A lot sweetie, but Scott is a great guy and won't do anything to hurt you."

"Yeah, I'm sure he won't," I say with sarcasm.

"Are you still going to Sido?"

"Yeah tonight. Just Alyssa and I, why?"

"Be careful, it's dangerous as you know."

"Yeah, so was living with you. I'm not that scared," I say walking back inside.

"I love you!"

I ignore her. Does she really love me? She didn't come over because she loves me, she came over because Mr. Washburn told her I was losing my shit. I walk back inside with more anger because Mr. Washburn had the nerve to tell my mom who I don't even associate with to come talk to me because "He's a nice guy."

"What an ass," I say out loud, so Mr. Washburn can hear me.

"You can get out of my damn house," he yells.

113

"Oh yeah, guess what, I will, you lying piece of shit."

"Dominic stop come back to my room," Alyssa says rushing out of her room grabbing me.

"I don't think I can stay here babe," I say shaking bad.

"Dominic, stay for me. Please."

"It's hard, I feel like my whole life has been surrounded by lies."

"Well I love you, that's not a lie."

Alyssa and I go back to her room, where we talk about everything that has happened and about our plan to go back to Sido tonight. It'll be risky but it's worth finding out the truth. Mr. and Mrs. Washburn don't have a clue that we're going tonight because they'd probably stop us. I look at my phone to see it's already seven o'clock.

"Are you ready?" Alyssa asks.

"Yeah, we're going to stop and get something to eat on our way there."

"Okay," she says getting up to go get the keys from her uncle.

She comes back in with a slight smile, "I told you I would get them."

I laugh and begin to soak everything in. On our way there we stop at Arby's so her and I don't pass out in the middle of the night. I savor the taste of my roast beef sandwich as Alyssa and I are approaching one of the most mysterious places in the world, hopefully for one of the last times. We pass the family park and airport. My heart begins to thump harder and faster each second that goes by. I look over at Alyssa and tell myself everything will be okay. Onto Stearns Point we go, then what feels like a second later we are stopping at Owen's Point. I take a deep breath and get out of the car.

"Remember the plan?" I ask.

"Yes," Alyssa says with a smile.

Alyssa and I head to the tunnel hoping it's still there. Sure enough, the tunnel Dr. Nunez created is still in existence. I hug Alyssa as her and I brace ourselves for what's next. But brace myself no more Alyssa jabs a needle into my stomach gently laying me on the ground as my vision begins to fade.

"I'm so sorry babe, I had too," she cries.

Before I go unconscious I feel someone pick me up. I look up to see it's Mr. Washburn. The last thing I hear is a voice that sounds like my mom telling Alyssa she did the right thing, and if she didn't go through with the plan, I could've ended up destroying the world.

# CHAPTER NINE

Betrayal, it never comes from your enemies, it comes from the people that you care most about. The ones that you'd take a bullet for. But this is something I've gotten used too. I had a feeling Alyssa would end up betraying me, too. I knew she would go back on everything she ever told me. I just wasn't expecting her betrayal to happen this soon. I guess Katherine Dobell was right, Dr. Hawkins is the only person I can trust. But where is he now?

  My eyes begin to open with foggy vision. I look around but there is nothing around me. When I look down I notice I'm tied down in a chair. I let out weak screams, but no one comes. The sweat pours onto my face causing a burning sensation in my eyes. Once my vision clears up a little more, I look around again. In each corner of the room there are cameras and in front of me there is a TV with a blank screen. Moments later, the TV comes on and what is shown is truly daunting. It shows the times Alyssa and I were together, and is replaying our conversations. It appears at times that she had a wire recording our conversations. Then without me ever knowing, they had cameras set up in her room. All those memories I felt were special, but to her it was all an act. The TV plays all my conversations with Mr. and Mrs. Washburn and my mom. Then suddenly, it shuts off, and Mr. Washburn comes through the door.

"Trippy, huh?" Mr. Washburn asks.

"You're a sick bastard."

"Oh yeah? Fuck you Dominic Wilkerson and your dead daddy too," he says punching me in the mouth with all of his strength.

Blood gushes everywhere and I dangle my head there for a couple seconds to recover.

"Damn, you're a bigger bitch than your deceased nephew," I say expecting to get hit again.

Mr. Washburn comes over to me and begins to choke me. Christine comes running through the door almost immediately.

"Scott! Get off him, you can't kill him yet," Christine yells.

He unlatches his arms that were around my neck, then he spits in my face. After Mr. Washburn leaves, Christine comes back in shooting a needle into my left arm. I scream in pain, but the pain only lasts for seconds before I'm knocked out into unconsciousness.

I open my eyes but this time my eyes aren't foggy. I'm no longer in the room by myself. I see a man approach me in all white.

"My son, come with me," the man says.

117

I follow him out of the room that I was held captive in wondering if I've died. My dad and I walk upstairs to where I see Mr. and Mrs. Washburn watching the cameras.

"This, my son, is an underground bunker. I came to you to show you where you are and how you can escape. Help will come your way in just a few hours so stay strong. At the end of all of this I want you to shut down Sido. There is documentation proving what Sido truly is and I want you to show it to the world. You'll live a better life than I did. Before I go I want you to know Alyssa truly didn't betray you, she had no other choice."

"Dad, please don't go."

"You'll be fine, I promise," he says disappearing into the distance.

My eyes shoot open and I'm still tied down in the chair. I look around, but everything is foggy again. Was that truly my dad in my dream? I've never been a firm believer in any form of afterlife but maybe there is such thing. What felt like hours later, Alyssa comes through the door. When she enters she locks the door behind her. She runs to me crying with a million apologizes.

"I never wanted to hurt you, but they threatened me," she cries.

"It'll be okay, I have help on the way," I whisper.

She looks up with a confused look. "How do you know?"

"My dad told me so."

"Dom, your dad is dead."

"Well, while I have been lying here unconscious, my dad came to me in a dream telling me that I'll be out of here in a few hours."

"You will be," she says hesitantly.

"How do you know?"

"Dom, you've been here for two days but they wanted to keep you asleep. The day after I did what I had to do, Dr. Hawkins comes out of nowhere grabbing me aside. He was there when I jabbed the needle into your stomach. He told me he didn't want to save you then because he wanted you to see what kind of people my Aunt and Uncle are. He also told me to tell you that he was sorry, he had no clue about your mom and was totally blindsided. Anyways, him and I came up with a plan to get you out of here. It could turn into a war, but they'll kill you otherwise. Let's just say he put together a team to come save you and afterwards this underground bunker may not exist," she whispers in my ear.

"How many people are going to try to save me?"

"Let's just say there's quite of few. I have to go, I love you."

"I love you, too," I say.

I wonder if they could hear everything she told me. But surely not or when she opens the door they'd hurt her. When she opens the door, Christine comes in. She takes a seat in front of me smiling.

"What do you want from me?" I ask in a calm manner.

119

"Truthfully, I want you to be reunited with your dad in hell. But I feel like as we're approaching your death I should tell you something about Mr. Washburn and I."

"What? That you and your husband are disgusting human beings?"

She laughs. "No, Scott and I work for people. Those people are why we want you dead."

"Who, the drug cartel?"

"No, your own government. Scott and I were put in this city, so nothing got out of hand. You're underground in the middle of nowhere right now. Surrounding you are more people that work for the government with high powered machinery."

"Bullshit, the government wouldn't hire a worthless piece of shit like you."

"Oh yeah? Then what do you call this?" she says showing me an official government identification badge.

"Look why do you guys want to kill me so bad? Why am I that important?"

"Dominic, I would tell you. You truly are important. But we need you dead because you're so young and would follow your dad's instructions and tell the whole world. Which can possibly cause the next World War, and we don't want that to happen."

"Look, I don't want to die, I'll do whatever you want, I'll move to Canada. I'll do whatever, I just want to live life."

"Sorry, Dominic, your dad has it written to make sure you show all documentation to the world since you'd be the only one that would know the truth and could make it public with sustainable evidence."

"Christine please, let me out of here!" I beg.

"I'm sorry Dominic, if I do that then I'll be killed," she says leaving the room.

At this point I hope Alyssa is really telling the truth about the plan to get me out of here. I was born into this world as an innocent child that becomes the centerpiece of some government bullshit. Just minutes after Christine leaves the room, my mom walks in.

"Hey, nobody that means anything to me," I say.

"Hey son, that is a miniature version of his shitty father."

"What's your connection?" I ask.

"The Washburns hired me years ago to take part in their operation," she says, while taking a seat across from me.

"So, your operation is to kill me?"

"Well yeah, that's about seventy-five percent of it."

"What the hell, what's wrong with you?"

"Your dad was a bad person, so I wanted to help."

"Bad person? Says the one that wants to have her own son killed."

"Well maybe if I loved you I wouldn't be trying to kill you."

"Why not kill me when I was younger?"

"Oh I wanted too, but the Washburns wanted you to be old enough to understand everything, so now, here we are.

"You've got to be kidding me. I'm done talking to you."

She gets up and walks out of the room. I'm in so much disbelief it's unreal. My whole life was a lie. All the I love you's were a lie. Literally, there hasn't been one thing in my life that has been real. Everything these psychotic people want to happen, happens.

∞ ∞ ∞

Mr. Washburn comes in the room again. This time he looks like he didn't come to talk shit.

"Hey Dominic, just came to put you asleep," he says jabbing a needle in my right arm.

I slowly fall asleep but this time instead of my dad approaching me, it's Bryan. He grabs my hand and tells me to come with him. He tells me to close my eyes. When I open them we're back in the city. There are helicopters flying all over, along with military vehicles sweeping the streets of Hot Springs.

"Your dad wasn't lying, there's people coming to save you."

"Why do you care? Aren't you one of them?"

"I didn't know anything, until the night I disappeared in Sido and found everything out. I was let go but one night in the middle of the night, I came home confronting my Aunt and Uncle about everything. They then beat the shit out of me, dropping me off somewhere. I was found and taken to the hospital. When they realized I was going to survive they made sure I didn't. I came to you that night that I died, telling you to run but you probably thought it was your imagination."

"Do you know everything?"

"Not until after I died, then my heavenly father told me everything. Let me just tell you, you're in for a lot of surprises."

"You can't tell me?"

"I'll tell you one thing. Those clues that you are getting, you obviously know it's Katherine Dobell. But Katherine Dobell changed her name. She died before you ever started getting clues, which means she wrote them out, knowing she'd die and then someone that's alive would deliver them. But damn, she has some sass, especially when you look at her up and down," he says with a wink.

"I don't get it."

"Well maybe at the end of this you will, don't think too hard. I'll see you again one day but not anytime soon."

He vanishes into thin air and everything goes black. My eyes jolt open after not being able to see anything for a couple of minutes. I hear explosions bursting above me. I now know what's going on. Part of me is excited, but another part of me is scared for what is to come. The rapid gunfire and rare explosions occur for hours. Then the door opens with a friendly face walking through, Dr. Hawkins.

"Hey buddy, I'm going to get you out of here."

He cuts the rope that held me to the chair. Then he lifts me up over his shoulder. I look at the chair that held me captive for several days. Tears of joy rush down my face, while he carries me up the stairs I already knew existed. He walks up multiple staircases until we are at the top. Once him and I are at the top, he walks over to an edge where there's light. We walk out of what seems like a tunnel to a helicopter. Dr. Hawkins lifts me into the helicopter and sits alongside me. He puts an aviation headset over my ears as we lift into the air.

"Look at the beauty of Hot Springs National Park. Good thing it isn't super dry here or there would be a wildfire from the explosives," Hawkins says laughing. I laugh a little wondering where life will take me now. What else will I find out?

"Hawkins, is Alyssa okay?"

"Yeah bud, she is waiting for you at the hospital."

I smile, excited to see her. It took no time to reach St. Vincent's. When the helicopter arrives, there is medical personnel waiting for me on top of the hospital. They put me onto a bed and rush me to a room. All the nurses are talking crazy, like I'm a celebrity. They get me into the room and I see my mom coming in the room.

"Mom? Get away now!"

Dr. Hawkins follows in behind her telling me to calm down and everything will be okay.

"Hey sweetie, how are you feeling?"

"Fine?"

A nurse comes in telling them to leave for a couple of minutes.

"Hi Dominic, I'm Nurse Andrews. I will be taking care of you. You're here for safety protocol. It's nothing serious, your body's just a little weak right now but you should be feeling great by the end of the night with all the IV's we give you. We'll keep you overnight just to make sure everything looks good. I have food on its way since it sounds like you haven't eaten in a couple of days. Do you have any questions for me?"

"No, sounds good. Can you send only that man back here please?"

"Will do."

Dr. Hawkins comes back to explain.

"Your mom worked for me, I told Alyssa to tell you that I was just as much blindsided because you needed to believe that your mom wanted you dead or the Washburns would wonder why you're not scared. So, I'm sorry about that, I heard it was pretty messed up. But Dominic, she honestly does love you."

"Can I see her?"

"Of course."

My mom comes back hesitantly, and sits down next to me.

"When will I know everything?"

"Well, right now there's no hurry to tell you everything. I know Katherine Dobell still has three clues left for you, so I think it'd be best for you to find out the way you were supposed to."

"What about the government? They're going to come for you, look what you guys just did. It's going to be the topic of every news story."

"They won't come for us. If they do, we'll give you the documentations to expose them which would turn into citizens turning against the government."

"Are you sure?"

"I'm positive."

"What's Sido? And why did people go missing?"

"I'm not going to tell you that. I'm pretty sure your father has a letter for you alongside the documents."

"Why can't you just tell me now," I plea.

"Your father wanted you to find out naturally so that's what's going to happen. Now if we were being threatened we would abandon that idea, but since everything is the best it's been in the last eighteen years, we're going to let it happen naturally."

"Okay, fine. Bryan came to me in one of my dreams and told me I'm in for a lot of surprises, is that true?"

She smiles and laughs. "Oh yes, ones that'll probably haunt you for the rest of your life. But we'll be here for you to get you through everything."

"Okay," I laugh. "Can I talk to Alyssa?"

"Yes, I'll go get her."

My mom leaves and before I knew it Alyssa was with me.

"I told you that we were going to save you," she says kissing me.

"What were your first intentions of being with me?" I ask.

"Well, I was told to get close to you, so I did. But then I did something I never expected and that was falling in love with the most amazing guy in the world."

"Aw, well I'm glad you did."

She smiles. "Oh yeah, I forgot I was supposed to bring this to you, it's clue five."

"So, are you Katherine's secret deliverer?"

"No," she laughs. "I believe that was your mom."

"Damn, that's crazy. Never would've thought."

"Hurry and open it."

"Hold on, can I ask you something first?"

"Sure."

"Who really brought me to the hospital and signed me in the last time I was here?"

"Your mom, why would you ever have believed what I said? You saw the video of her but just to get you thinking more she signed in as me."

"Were you guys close to Nunez?"

"I wasn't ever around her, but your mom was and they orchestrated a lot of this."

I open clue five ready to expect the unexpected.

*"Dominic,*

*I know it's been a rocky road and I wish I could be there for you. If you already haven't figured it out I was killed by the Washburns. Right now, I don't have much to say to you except I'm sorry for not being there. I had to make sure everything happened the way your father wanted it too. This isn't as much of a clue as it is an apology. I love you little brother." -Katherine Dobell*

# CHAPTER TEN

Flashing back throughout my whole life, I now see it all wasn't lies. My mom truly does love me, Alyssa never wants to lose me, and Nunez was never against me. The more time that goes by, the more I'm allowed to figure out. Yet, there is one thing really bothering me. At the end of clue five, Katherine Dobell said, "I love you little brother." To my knowledge I have no other siblings, but at this point I wouldn't be surprised if I really did. I turn on the TV to find breaking news about the explosions in the National Park. The headline caption is, "Chaos erupts in National Park, who's responsible?" Luckily, the news will have a hard time figuring out what truly happened. Dr. Hawkins walks into my room with a smile.

"How are you feeling?"

"Eh, about as good as ever."

"We'll get you out of here tomorrow."

"What happens if the news, broadcasts what really happened?"

"They won't, I already have it setup to believe it's a chemical explosion."

"But I'm sure people seen the military sweeping the city."

"True. But trust me, it'll never be known to anyone that shouldn't know."

"Whatever you say."

"I'll let you get some sleep, I'll see you in the morning," he says.

"Goodnight," I say.

I dream of nothing for once. It was a bittersweet feeling to not feel awake when I'm asleep. When I wake up in the morning, my mom, Alyssa, and Hawkins are in the room.

"Take me home already," I say laughing.

"Good Morning to you, too," Hawkins says.

Nurse Andrews comes in my room to make sure it's okay for me to leave.

"You're all set, do you think you can walk on your own?"

"Totally, watch!"

I get out of my bed and as soon as I try taking my first step my legs give out on me. I sit there kind of embarrassed.

"Wow, impressive," Hawkins says.

"Let me get you a wheelchair," Nurse Andrews exclaims.

"Oh no, that's not needed. I'll carry him to the car," Hawkins says.

Hawkins lifts me onto his back once again, carrying me out to the car. Alyssa sits in the back with me. Not much was said on the way back to my mom's, she just lies her head on my chest. When we arrive home, Hawkins carries me inside and lays me down gently on the couch.

"Can I go to my room instead?" I ask.

"No, your mom and I want to talk to you. Alyssa can stay with you though."

"Okay. After we talk, can I go back there?"

"Yeah, if that's okay with your mom."

"It is," she says.

"Okay, your mom and I want to tell you we are here for you no matter what. I'll be staying here and sleeping on the couch for your protection. If you have questions that you don't understand, her and I will do our best to give you clarity," Hawkins says.

"Sounds good. I do have a question for my mom."

"What's that?" She asks.

"In clue five, Katherine addressed me as her little brother. Is she my sister?"

"Well, I do know the answer. But I feel like you should find out on your own as it'll be disclosed in clue seven."

"So, what's the point of asking you guys questions if you guys are just going to give me this "Everything will be known naturally bullshit."

"I should've said, we'll answer any concerns to your well-being."

"Ah I see. I guess I'm done here, can someone help me to my room?"

This time Hawkins helps me to my room instead of carrying me. I lay on my bed and realize it's been a long time since I've been here. Alyssa and I are happy we still get to be together. Not to long after I get to my room my mom comes rushing in.

"By the way, I have no grandkids and I'd like to keep it that way," she laughs.

"Okay, Mom," I smile.

She then goes into the kitchen to prepare lunch. I stare at the ceiling not sure what to make of everything that's going on.

"Are you scared?" Alyssa asks.

"Not really, I feel protected with those around me."

"You're not even scared of the truth?"

"Eh, a little but I know I have you and you'll get me through whatever I find out."

"Okay good, I don't want you to be scared."

"Do you know everything?" I ask curiously.

"I believe so, but I promised I wouldn't tell you."

"It's okay, I don't want you to tell me. I just want you to be by my side forever."

"And forever and ever," she says.

Her and I lay in bed until my mom calls us for lunch.

"Hey, you two. I made fettuccine alfredo for lunch," says my mom.

Alyssa and I sit down at the table. We hold hands as Dr. Hawkins prays before we eat. I dig in as soon as we say amen. Oh, how have I missed my mom's cooking. It feels like I ate it all in a few bites. Before I dismiss myself from the table, I make sure everyone else is done eating. Once Alyssa finishes, I grab her plate and clean it off and stick it into the dishwasher. Alyssa and I go back to my room and relax for the rest of the day. I find myself with my eyes closed unable to wake up. After fighting, trying to wake up, I eventually give up and that's when Dr. Nunez, Bryan, and my dad come to me.

"Follow us," Nunez says.

I follow her knowing this is all just a dream. I'm at peace with myself since I'm surrounded by the people I want back in my life. They take me to Sido and explain things I never knew.

"Son, this is what I have created. I believed I was doing the right thing for our country," my dad says.

"What happened?" I ask.

"I should not tell you yet since I have a letter written for you in a safe. Also in that safe is documentation showing what this country has become."

"How do I get the safe?"

"After you discover Clue seven your mom and Hawkins will direct you to what needs to happen next."

"What about all the missing people?"

"Sido wasn't created to abduct people, but that also is explained in my letter to you."

Nunez grabs my hand. "Dominic, you're in good care, nothing bad will happen to you. At this point your government is afraid of you."

"So you guys promise all my questions will be answered with no more confusion?"

"We promise your questions will be answered but I'm sure confusion will still exist."

"Alright," I say knowing this dream won't last forever.

"Before we let you go, let us explain. Our world is more divided than ever, our hope is to unify this country and come together no matter your beliefs or your appearance. The government created this division in people for one purpose and that purpose will later be explained. Goodbye, Dominic."

I wake up with Alyssa laying on my chest. I kiss her on her forehead, gently lying her head on a pillow. I walk out of my room to talk to Hawkins. I find him and my mom talking on the back deck. I peek my head outside of the sliding door.

"Hawkins, may I talk to you?"

"Of course." he says walking inside.

Hawkins and I take a seat on the couch. I'm a little nervous to talk about dead people coming into my dreams.

"Recently, when I sleep, I've been having dreams of Bryan, Nunez, and my dad coming to me. Is that normal?"

He smiles and grabs my hand. "Dominic, these dreams are often referred to as, "Visitation Dreams." It's totally normal but I wouldn't refer to them as dreams at all. They're actually coming to you, and it's very real. Whatever they tell you, it's to comfort you. Appreciate these, because once this is all over they will become more rare."

"They told me this is about the government trying to divide us. Is that true?"

"Partially, but the reason why they want us divided is the bigger answer. The way they are trying to divide us can simply be based on one's income. That's just an example, it's bigger than that."

"Why am I involved? I'm only seventeen-years-old. I don't know a damn thing about the government."

"You don't need too. The only reason you're a part of this is because this is how your dad has it to happen. Like I've said already, stay calm and you'll get everything you want soon."

"Will you please just tell me one thing?"

"What's that?"

"Is Katherine Dobell my sister?"

"You have to promise not to say anything because I promised I wouldn't tell you anything."

"I promise I won't say anything to anyone."

"Yes, Katherine Dobell is your sister," Hawkins whispers.

∞ ∞ ∞

My whole life I always wanted a brother or sister. Little did I know, I had a sister that I will never get to meet. She has yet to come to me in one of my dreams, but I hope one day I'll get to see her. After Hawkins went back to talk to my mom I sat there in disbelief. Had she never run away when she was younger, would her and I have grown up together? She obviously lived after she went missing when she was younger but her true death will always be unknown. I don't know what hurts more. Not ever getting to see her or not being able to visit her grave because no one knows she lived years and years after her disappearance. Also, my last questions about Katherine are, was it my mom or dads kid and what's her true identity?

Alyssa comes out in the living room as I watch news coverage of the "National Park Disaster." The news coverage talks about how there was an explosion caused by piping underground. Even though that isn't the case the city had to be paid a lot of money to lie.

"What actually happened to your parents?" I ask Alyssa curiously.

"They were killed when Bryan and I were younger."

"I know that, but do you know what happened?"

"Yes," she frowns.

"Sorry, I won't ask about it, if it's uncomfortable to talk about."

"No, it's okay. When I was four years old my parents were killed in their own house. Bryan and I at the time were in school. We lived in Baltimore. Bryan and I were told that our house was robbed and sadly our parents tried fighting off the robbers. I always thought that was the truth until years ago. My aunt and uncle told Bryan and I what really happened. They told us that my parents worked for the government and they didn't see eye to eye on something, so they were killed and Bryan and I were given to my Aunt and Uncle. Now, I believe the disagreement between my parents and the government was exactly what my Aunt and Uncle did when they moved us here and built an underground bunker to fight Sido. My parents were trying to look out for our safety but then they lost their own lives. I only have vague memories of them, but since then life hasn't been the same. The greatest thing that I was never expecting was being with you. As painful as the past has been, I would never take back meeting you in a million life times."

Listening to her, I am filled with mixed emotions. When she tells me everything, I can feel the pain and that brought me to tears. Her and I share one thing, and that is the darkness in our lives. It's like her and I were chosen to live these lives while others get to live fearless.

"I can promise you one thing. From here until eternity, no one can separate us or keep us from being happy. You are the light in my darkness even on the darkest days of my life," I say.

"Aw Dominic, I love you," she says leaping into my arms with happy tears streaming down her face.

Then a knock at the door interrupts our conversation. I walk down the stairs to the door and find another package, that I assume is clue six. I take it back upstairs and take a seat next to my mom and Hawkins on the deck.

"Mom, I know you are the one that was delivering the clues, why didn't you just hand this to me yourself?"

"Honey, I have clue six in my room, that isn't it."

"What do you mean? I refuse to open this, it could be a bomb from the government."

"No, stop, it's not from the government. I'll open it with you," Hawkins says.

Hawkins and I simultaneously open it, seeing that it isn't a bomb. Instead, it's a letter from Bryan.

*"Dear Dominic,*

*Please take care of my sister and never let her go. I want to look down on you one day from above saying, "That's my brother in law." I want to apologize for how this all has happened. You're a good guy with a good heart. Before we went to Sido, I put the ring my mom wore in a box for you to give to Alyssa. One day when you feel the time is right, I want you to give this ring to Alyssa. This ring is all I had left of my mom. With this ring, I want you to promise me that you'll be there for Alyssa no matter what. Also, when you put this ring on her finger I want you to promise to take care of her until you die. I know this seems strange, but I wasn't sure that night if I would make it out alive and if you're reading this, then I'm gone, but my spirit will always be with you." -Bryan*

Hawkins read it along with me. Him and I both were hit with emotions while reading the letter. I look at the bottom of the package to see a ring box. I open the box to see a ring, sitting there with a shiny reflection.

"I told you it wasn't a bomb," Hawkins says.

"Umm, isn't this too soon?"

"Bryan didn't tell you when to give it to her."

"I think I'm going to wait a little longer."

"There's nothing wrong with that."

I hear Alyssa come out of my bedroom, so I close the box sticking it and the letter into my pocket. I hand the packaging to Hawkins, so he can throw it away. My mom comes inside shutting the sliding door behind her. About the time my mom gets in the kitchen so does Alyssa.

"Hey honey I have something for you," my mom says to me.

"Okay?"

She leaves the room for a couple of minutes.

"Hey babe," I say.

"What was the knock on the door for?"

"It was for me, some scam bullshit," Hawkins says coming into the kitchen.

"Oh, okay."

My mom comes back in the kitchen and hands me a package.

"Clue six?" I ask.

"Yes."

I walk into the living room where I open clue six alone. I begin to get anxious opening the packaging not knowing what I'll find out now.

*"Dominic,*

*It's been a journey to get you where you stand. Everyone is so close to the truth but in the end, it'll be your decision. I have told you things I felt like you needed to know. The whole reason I decided to do these clues was, so you wouldn't feel like you're alone. The first clues I created I felt like were actual clues. These last couple I feel like is more about telling you the truth. So, this clue I want to tell you this. Your dad and my mom are how I was created. Sidney disappeared as a disguise to make it look like Sido was a mystery. Your dad sent Sidney away for her safety. The last thing you need to know you'll find out in the last clue. I love you."*

*-Katherine Dobell*

I walk back into the kitchen ready for clue seven.

"Surprised?" My mom asks.

"Nothing surprises me anymore."

They all laugh and look at me like I'm crazy.

"Let me tell you, don't say that. The truth will blow your mind," Hawkins says.

"My mind is already blown."

"Whatever you say."

"By the way I ordered pizzas and they should be here shortly," my mom says.

Alyssa and I lay on the couch while waiting for the pizza.

"I can't do anything but smile when I look at you," I say.

"Why's that?"

"Because I can't believe how lucky I am to be able to call you mine."

"Well, I am yours and that will never change."

The door rings with the delivery guy at the door with our pizzas. For once in my life as we eat together, everything feels right. Smiles and laughter overcome all the fears of what's to happen. Yet, the unknown is still to come.

# CHAPTER ELEVEN

The journey to discovering the truth is approaching with every second that goes by. The past weeks have been a roller coaster of emotions, but I wouldn't give it up for the world because of the amazing people that have been by my side. I never could have expected any of this to happen to me. It all started with a fight that led me to the principal's office. From there, Nunez was able to ask me to go to Sido with her. That one day has led to this journey of secrets, truths, and lies. It's opened my eyes to see who my family, friends, and enemies are.

Hawkins woke Alyssa and I up early to get clothes for Bryan's wake later tonight. My mom arranged to have Bryan's wake at the same church Nunez's funeral was held. Hawkins has Alyssa and I buy whatever we want for his wake and funeral so her and I look nice.

"Hey Hawkins, what happened to the police trying to find you?" I ask, while checking out at the store.

"That whole ordeal was all planned by myself and the police."

"So, no one is looking for you?"

"No, people don't look for you when you give them what they want."

"Ah, I see."

After Alyssa and I get our clothes, Hawkins takes us to breakfast at Megan's Diner. The same diner where I was watching the news when my mom called in that I went missing.

"Why did my mom file me as missing?"

"Everything that happened was to keep you thinking. None of us wanted you to get comfortable with anything so we continually had to throw curve balls your way. It was all preparation for what's to come. We figured, if you're always thinking then in the end it'll be easier for you to handle the truth."

Arriving at Megan's Diner I feel this time it should be a much better experience. Alyssa and I sit next to each other in a booth while Hawkins sits across from us. I look at the menu and decide since everything is changing in my life why not make a change on what I order. Instead of ordering the Ultimate Omelette, I decide to order the Banana Split Pancakes. The breakfast felt much like last night while eating dinner. It brings a feeling that I can't even explain, I just know it's a good feeling. Hawkins is a man of many jokes that would bring a smile to anyone's face. Deep down I have the uneasy feeling of life ahead of me, but I try to keep myself calm with those around me.

"Hey, when we get home, do you want to go on a walk?" I ask Alyssa.

"I'd love too."

Once finished eating, Hawkins gets a to go omelette for my mom. When we leave the diner, I look around me and smile. The drive home was a quick one since Hawkins likes to drive thirty over all the speed limits, which I don't blame him because it seems like he can get away with anything. I don't even go inside when we get home, I grab Alyssa's hand as her and I go for a walk.

"Are you okay?" Alyssa asks.

"Yeah, why?"

"Just making sure."

I take Alyssa back to the spot where everything took off that day by the river. It's where I ran into her, but looking at it now, she is the one that, found me. In my unspoken past, I have been hurt, but she lays any pain I ever have had to rest. Her and I take a seat on a bench close to the edge of the river. I stare beyond, at the beautiful view from the bench, where I see nothing but a bright future for myself. Alyssa and I sit there for hours enjoying the peace and quiet. I question myself, if I should give her the ring Bryan gave to me, right now. But if yesterday was too soon, then what makes today any different? After hours spent at the river, Alyssa and I head back to my house. When Alyssa and I get home, Hawkins and my mom are nowhere to be found. I look at the time seeing it's almost noon. I go back to my room to find my clothes along with Alyssa's sitting on my bed.

"I forgot about those," I say laughing.

I throw the clothes on the floor as Alyssa and I lay on the bed talking about everything that has happened and my anticipation of what is to come. She tries to calm my anxiety about the future by rubbing my back, which apparently worked because I'm awoke by the sound of a car door being shut. I jump up and look out the window to see my mom and Hawkins. I run into the kitchen to see it's already six and the wake begins at seven-thirty. Before Hawkins and my mom get inside I wake Alyssa up. When they walk through the door I jump into the shower making it look like I'm getting ready. I take the quickest shower of my life knowing Alyssa needs to get in here as soon as possible since it will take her longer to get ready. When I open the bathroom door, Alyssa rushes in and takes her shower. I quickly throw on a t-shirt and shorts, then I walk into the living room where Hawkins looks at me.

"Have a little too much fun while we were gone?"

"Hawkins, don't even start with me."

He laughs. "It's okay, I remember being that age too. Just appreciate being young while you can, because in a blink of an eye you'll be looking like me."

"If life goes by this slow like it has in the past couple weeks, it'll be forever before I look like you."

"Trust me, after this is over, time will pass without you even knowing. Then all the sudden you'll have a family, a job, and living the American Dream."

I think about what I'm going to do with my life after all of this, all I know is I plan on going to college. I go back to my room to put my dress clothes on as seven-thirty is approaching fast. I look into my dresser mirror to make sure I look good in my American Eagle apparel. I comb my hair to the way I desire and walk back out in the living room.

"How do I look?"

"You look like you're going to a fashion show," Hawkins says.

"Roger, stop. You look very handsome, Dominic," my mom says.

"Thanks, Mom."

Alyssa goes back to my room to get ready, so we can get to the wake on time. If she looked as good as she did the other night, I know she'll look even better tonight. When Alyssa comes out she looks stunning in a casual blue dress that brings out the color in her beautiful blue eyes. Her dress is knee length, which shows her long tan legs. She looks at me with a smile.

"Do I look okay?" She asks.

"You look like the most beautiful girl in this world," I respond.

She comes over to me and puts her arm around my waist. She is almost as tall as me in her wedged black sandals. I put my arms around her, grabbing her close for a kiss. Under different circumstances this would have been a great moment, but the reality hits both of us as Alyssa chokes back tears.

"I can't believe he's gone."

I hold her tightly as tears begin to flow down her face. I begin to get teary eyed as well, but I know I must be strong for Alyssa. Hawkins yells at us from downstairs.

"Are you guys ready?"

"Let's go," I say.

Hawkins gets us to the church in what felt like just a matter of seconds. I stay with Alyssa at the wake as I get to meet the side of her family that's not evil. I look around to see there is no pictures or videos of Bryan playing on the screen that stands behind his body.

"No pictures of Bryan?" I ask Alyssa.

"No," she says sadly.

"Why?"

"There are none. My aunt and uncle didn't care to document our lives as we got older. All they cared about was one thing, which resulted in their deaths."

The only picture was a big picture of Bryan in his high school football uniform that stood by his casket. Although, there wasn't any memories of Bryan, the wake was well organized, with the help of my mom and some of Bryan's family from Baltimore. Alyssa didn't want to be a part of that, because she would get too emotional. After meeting her family, I take a seat in the corner reminiscing on everything Bryan and I went through. Finally, I take a deep breath and approach where his body lies with an open casket. I hesitantly look over the edge to see his lifeless young body with his hands folded over one another. Tears pour from my eyes knowing these are the last days I'll ever see him. I glance at him one last time, and it was as if he came alive just to say one last word.

"Promise?"

∞ ∞ ∞

Emotions rise as the funeral nears. A storm rolls in as I wake up from a dead sleep. Alyssa is already getting ready for Bryan's funeral, which begins at noon. I grab my suit and tie that I got yesterday with Hawkins and lay it out across my bed. I take a quick shower and eat breakfast as this gloomy day is only to get gloomier. I go in my room after I finish eating breakfast to start putting on my dress clothes. Hawkins comes in once I have everything on to tie my tie. I look at myself in the mirror, spraying cologne across my suit. I walk into the living room where everyone awaits me.

"Looking sharp kiddo," Hawkins says.

"Not too bad yourself." I reply.

Again, Alyssa is looking amazing wearing a darker blue dress than she did yesterday. Like a family, we head out the door. Hawkins couldn't get us there so quick today because of the morning traffic, but we are still the first to arrive, along with some of Bryan's other family that has helped organize the funeral. I sit down on the sofa and just stare at the wall with a million thoughts running through my head. After an hour, people begin to show up, including classmates I go to school with. Bryan's funeral is more of an open funeral whereas Nunez's was more of an intimate family memorial. I head into the seating area, taking a seat in the second row since the first is reserved for family. When the clock strikes noon, it's a packed church and the pastor comes in to give an opening prayer. I sit there alongside Hawkins and my mom, and Alyssa is in the row in front of me. I listen to the same things that I heard just a few days ago when I came to Nunez's funeral. I catch myself a couple different times with my eyes closed but look around each time to make sure no one seen me. Everyone is looking straight into the direction of the pastor with tears pouring out their eyes. I close my eyes again and when I open them I look up feeling like the world is spinning. I look over at my mom, but I can't concentrate and I begin to freak out. I don't want to cause any commotion because that would be embarrassing so I sit there for a couple of minutes trying to fight it. With a couple minutes that go by, it only gets worse, so I stand up and try to get out of the aisle quietly. Once

I get to the doors, I gently push them open and find the nearest bathroom. I go into a stall and immediately vomit into the toilet. I try to breathe, but I have trouble catching my breath. I take toilet paper to clean my mouth and just lie against the stall. Eventually I regain my breath and everything around me slowly begins to stop spinning. I hold my hand over my heart to feel it thumping, rapidly. I lie there until my heart rate calms down. When I get up, my legs feel weak, but I flush the toilet behind me and return to the remainder of the service. I must've missed more of the service than I thought, because the service was over just minutes after I take a seat.

"How long was I gone?" I whisper to Hawkins.

"Long enough to miss the whole damn thing."

I remember Alyssa was giving a short speech, so I figure she'll be upset I wasn't there for that. Everyone stands up for a closing prayer then we depart out the doors. I head to the car with my stomach aching for food. Alyssa comes up and bumps me into the wall.

"Are you okay babe?" She asks.

"I think I had an anxiety attack."

She grabs my hand and goes in for a kiss.

"You don't want to kiss me. I threw up in the bathroom," I say backing away from her lips.

"Do you feel good enough to go to the burial?"

"Yes, I want to be there with you."

Her and I get into the back of the car as Hawkins follows the hearse being escorted by motorcycle cops to the cemetery. After a lengthy drive, we finally arrive at Greenwood Cemetery, where Bryan will be laid to rest. The preacher reads a short committal speech.

"Believing in the Resurrection to eternal life through our Lord Jesus Christ, we now entrust Bryan Washburn to the care of our Almighty God and we ask our Father to open the doors to his mansion and lead Bryan to the room made ready just for him. As we now commit his body to the ground, the deep, the elements, its final resting place; earth to earth, ashes to ashes, dust to dust, we commend his spirit to its new home. Rest eternal grant him; and let light perpetual shine upon him."

I look around me seeing guys from afar dressed in black with shades looking through binoculars right where we stand. I tap Hawkins on the side and point in the direction of where the men are standing.

"They're with us. Before the funeral, I was told to take extra precautionary measures," Hawkins whispers.

"From what?"

"My sources told me that the government may try to pull some shenanigans, so I didn't want to take any chances."

"What are they going to do? Shoot the government with their binoculars?"

"No, I have a team of snipers set across the cemetery."

"That sounds real peaceful," I joke.

We leave the cemetery after Bryan's casket is lowered into the ground. The clouds begin to come together making it feel like there will be another storm. Once Hawkins drives away so does all the black SUV's that surrounded us. Alyssa looks out the window with tears. I grab her and pull her close to me.

"It's finally over with," she says.

"He's in a better place," I whisper.

I comfort her on our way home still feeling a little nauseous. When Hawkins pulls into the driveway Alyssa is asleep on my shoulder. I get out of the car and gently pick her up to carry her inside. After I get inside I lay her on my bed and rush to the bathroom to brush my teeth. I take three swigs of mouthwash just to make sure my mouth is disinfected. I go into the kitchen to make a sandwich to give my stomach some food. After I get myself feeling better I take off my suit, feeling more relaxed. I go back into my room and lay next to my beautiful girlfriend. She wakes up not long after I lay down.

"Did you brush your teeth?" She asks.

I laugh. "Yes."

"Good," she says as we kiss.

"Let me go take this dress off, I'll be back."

"Are you sure you don't want me to do it for you?" I smirk.

She smiles. "I'll be back."

When she comes back she looks amazing even without makeup with her brown curly hair pulled back into a ponytail, dressed in sweats and a t-shirt.

"What?" I ask.

"I just wonder how I got so lucky."

"Lucky? I'm the one that's lucky."

"You're a dream that is my reality," she says.

She leans in and her and I begin to kiss, then my mom comes in my room to tell us dinner is done. After I get up, I notice my stomach feeling weird again, but nothing could bother me because I was with the one person that made all my worries go away. Alyssa and I go to the dinner table with country fried steak, mashed potatoes, and corn on the table.

We pass everything around and pray before we eat.

Hawkins begins the prayer, "Our Father, which art in heaven, hallowed be thy name. Thy Kingdom come. Thy will be done on earth, as it is in heaven. Give us this day our daily bread. And forgive us our trespasses, as we forgive them that trespass against us. And lead us not into temptation, but deliver us from evil. For thine is the kingdom, the power, and the glory, For ever and ever. Amen."

Throughout the prayer, I flashback to the night where Nunez gave this exact prayer outside of Sido. My throat begins to get dry and my palms become sweaty. When I open my eyes, the world spins again, with my heart rate rising. I get up, bumping the table and run into the bathroom to vomit once again. I sit hunched over the toilet until my mom comes in.

"What's wrong honey?"

"This is the second time I puked today."

She reaches into the cabinet above the toilet and hands me a pill.

"What's this?"

"It'll help you stop puking."

I flush the toilet and brush my teeth again to get the nasty taste out of my mouth. I go into the kitchen pouring a glass of water to take the pill. I take a seat and begin to slowly eat my food, but nothing sounds good.

"Did you give him medicine?" Hawkins asks my mom.

"Yeah, hopefully it'll help."

When I get done eating, I clean off my plate and throw myself on the bed feeling exhausted. Alyssa comes in and lays next to me.

"Feeling better?" She asks.

"Kind of."

Alyssa begins to cuddle up against me, but shortly after, my mom calls me into the living room. Alyssa grabs my hand tight while walking into the living room. Hawkins and my mom sit there with a package in the middle of the coffee table. I take a seat next to my mom and Alyssa sits close to me.

"This is it, clue seven. This will only be the beginning of what's to come but it's important that you read this. Are you ready?" My mom asks.

"Yeah, I guess."

"Before you open it, would you like to read it alone or with all of us?"

"Can Alyssa just be with me?"

"Yes," my mom says handing me the last clue, then heads to the kitchen.

My hands shake trying to open the package. I take out the folded piece of paper and unfold it.

*"Dominic,*

*This is it, the last clue. The first clue, I mentioned the town as having more secrets than the CIA because your dad worked for the CIA. From there you figured out I was Katherine Dobell, but I also talked about living in disguise. The clues kept you guessing and later you found out that I'm your sister. Throughout, I talked about you finding the truth in the end of clue seven. You may start thinking I just told you things and the truth at the end of this is that I lied about everything but that isn't the case. Everything I said is true, from when I said that you're being watched, to me saying that I love you. Before I get any further, I want to explain what's to come. After you read this, your mom will direct you to a safe that only you can get into with your fingerprint. The safe should be in your mom's possession and it holds all the documentation of what really happened in Sido. The reason you were the key all along is because you're the only person that can get into that safe because your dad wanted it that way. From there it's your decision on what to do with the documentation. Whether you want to tell the world, burn it, or keep it for retaliation later down the road. Your dad has it in there what he would want you to do but he died years ago from cancer. Hawkins was next in line to take control of Sido since he's your dad's brother. See, you never knew it, but you and I have met. I interacted with you a lot, whether that was taking you to Sido, showing you video footage, or stalking you at McDonalds. I believe you'll make the right choice. I love you."*

 *-Katherine Dobell A.K.A. Dr. Nunez*

# CHAPTER TWELVE

Haunted by the memories that will only exist in my mind. All along I questioned why Dr. Nunez, a successful woman that was the assistant principal of Hot Springs High School would give up everything for me. Now it makes more sense when I look back at everything. The clues were all there, but I wasn't in the state of mind to be able to see it. I know for however this is to end I will not be alone with the amazing people around me and most of all the three guardian angels watching over me.

I walk into the kitchen hugging my mom and Hawkins. My mind still hasn't been able to process the truth, but I know those around me will be there for me. Nothing ever suggested to me that Dr. Nunez could be my sister. I think about the years of thinking she was this mean person, but her and I were siblings.

"What is to happen now?" I ask Hawkins.

"Get a good night's rest, you'll know more tomorrow," Hawkins replies.

I walk to my room with the comfort of Alyssa. I jump under the covers and stare at the wall.

"I'm sorry I could never tell you," Alyssa says.

"Don't be sorry, all that matters is having you with me."

"Goodnight Dom."

"Goodnight," I say shutting my eyes.

When I wake up the thunder rumbles through the city. I lay there wondering if last night was all a dream. That theory is quickly debunked when I reach into my pocket to re-read clue seven. Throughout the clue a lot of things are discovered, but nothing hits me more than the ending. I hear Hawkins and my mom in the kitchen, so I decide to join them. I walk into the kitchen, heading over to the table and just sitting there completely still.

"Do you want to talk about it?" Hawkins asks.

"Yeah, Uncle Hawkins, let's talk about it."

"Why are you mad?" My mom asks.

"Sorry, my mind just can't grasp everything."

"Look, Dominic," Hawkins says sitting down. "It's okay to be upset, trust me I was upset too, when she died, but we can't redo the past. Besides, there is more for you to know."

"The only reason I'm upset is because I was rude to her. I hated seeing her, but now I'd do anything to have another conversation with her." I say.

My mom leaves, going into the other room. I continue to sit there with my head down in silence. My mom comes back with a big iron safe.

"Woah, don't hurt yourself," Hawkins says helping her set it on the table.

"Okay, whenever you want more, put your thumb on the pad and it will open."

"How does this have my fingerprint?"

"Dom, trust me it does. It's a lot easier than you think," Hawkins says.

"Can I open it now?"

"It's up to you buddy."

I stick my thumb on the pad and suddenly it unlocks. I slowly open the safe but once I do there is nothing but envelopes.

"Where do I start?"

"Here, I'll help you, you don't need to read them all because a lot of them aren't that important. There's just certain ones you should read now, then later when you get bored you can read the others. I know there's quite of few letters and things like that," Hawkins says.

Hawkins sorts out all the envelopes handing me the ones to read. Each of the envelopes are labeled so I know what it'll be talking about. The first one I open is labeled, *"Sidney Dobell."*

*"Sidney Dobell, a seventeen-year-old girl that went "missing" on July 7th, 1997. Sidney was with a "friend" the day*

159

she vanished by the Ouachita River. Her friend Jamie knew nothing about what was to happen, Sidney told her she wanted to run away so Jamie made up a story about the river like she was told. From there I sent Sidney to a safe house in Washington D.C. as they oathed to protect her. Then I faked my own disappearance and the government operation Sido (Secret Intelligence Defense Organization) would be underway. Sidney Dobell's location to this day is still unknown but last I heard the government had her detained."

After I read this it intrigues me to continue reading the rest of the envelopes. I sit there wondering for what else there is to know. I grab the next envelope that is labeled, *"Sido"*

*"Sido, a place that became the most mysterious place on earth. Tourists came from everywhere to attempt to find out what was happening. Most people believed it was a supernatural force capturing the souls of the people. That supernatural force was the government. Sido was initially supposed to be a hidden underground bunker that no other country knew about that created destructive forces such as advanced weaponry in preparation for the next world war. For the first years of Sido's existence this seemed true until it was leaked to me that, that wasn't the case. Sido was built for the next civil war that was being created by the government. From there, once a civil war broke out the government would unleash chemical weapons throughout the cities depleting the population and poor people. Why? This is what I asked myself until*

*I found out the government would show other countries that another epidemic has struck the United States. This would make other countries give money to help attempt to save the lives of the American people. Then they would use that money for treatments for the wealthy allowing the less fortunate to die and pocketing the rest of the money. The civil war was just to keep the people divided so they wouldn't unify and turn against the government."*

I get done reading and turn to Hawkins.

"Is this still to take effect?"

"It was but in the last years everything has become chaotic and the government backed down as long as no one apart of the operation releases the documents. Then they learned about you and now it's alarming others."

"So, I should just burn these documents?"

"No, I would keep them just in case."

"Don't the people deserve to know?"

"That's what your dad believed."

I move on to the next envelope that's labeled, *"Disappearances."*

*"The disappearances gave great disguise to what was really happening. It's kind of like when a big world event is happening but suddenly something else happens, directing our attention away from the big picture. The same method was used for Sido. People would visit Sido to discover the mystery, but the government made them disappear. I had nothing to do with any of that as that was done by*

161

*other government officials. My job was to build an underground*
*military empire while it was portrayed to be a supernatural place."*

"I think I need a break, this is weird shit."

"Yes it is, but it's the truth that lies behind everything that's
happened.

"Why couldn't this have been in preparation of the
apocalypse and aliens were behind all of this."

"Dominic, I know it's strange. But you need to know."

"So, it's all over money?"

"You need to keep reading."

I open the next envelope that is labeled, *"My Son."*
*"My son,*

*I know this is all strange and overwhelming, but I want to
bring you the truth. My advice is to share this with the world, so
everyone knows the truth. Some say you doing this will end the
world, but I believe this will save us all from any further human
extinction probabilities. I hope you make the right decision in the
end as I won't be there to guide you."*

"What should I do?"

"I will not push a decision on you, I'd say go with your gut."

Alyssa comes out sitting next to me trying to calm me down.

"Babe what should I do?" I whisper.

"Do what your heart tells you."

"Dammit none of you will tell me what to do!"

"Listen to your father," my mom says appearing from the living room.

∞ ∞ ∞

I decide not to jump to any decisions on what to do. Instead, I retreat to my room to be alone to think about the pro's and cons of the situation. I begin to feel overwhelmed knowing the future of the world is in my hands. I start to get angry wondering why my dad would put this responsibility on me. After all I'm only seventeen! I'm startled by a knock at my door.

"Dominic, are you okay?" Alyssa asks.

"Yes babe."

She slowly opens the door.

"Can I come in?"

"Of course."

Alyssa walks in and sees the distress on my face. She comes over to me and gives me a hug. Having her in my arms is the one thing that will always calm me down. I then start talking to her, but we're interrupted by a knock at the door.

"Dom, come to the living room," my mom says.

I grab Alyssa's hand and together her and I walk into the living room. I take a seat and look at my mom, wondering why I'm out here.

"Hawkins and I are wondering if you'd like us to take you to Sido?" My mom asks.

163

"Like right now?"

"Yes, like right now."

"Okay let me get dressed," I say kind of excited.

I go back to my room where Alyssa and I get ready in no time. Then we all head out the door. I begin to feel a little anxious of what awaits me at Sido. But with no second thoughts, I get in the car.

"Okay Dominic I want to explain something that your dad probably forgot," Hawkins says.

"Okay?"

"The location of Sido was purposely picked. It allowed for the shipments of weapons to be carried out on water instead of the streets. This was to prevent any speculation of the military being involved."

"I guess that's smart?"

"Also, when we get there don't touch anything."

When we arrive, we're in front of a building that's just in front of the electric fence. A building I never knew that existed but I'm assuming it leads to the underground portion of Sido.

I walk up the steps of the building as there are FBI agents everywhere along with the military. Hawkins explains to me that the FBI works for the government and the military is there so the FBI don't attempt anything out of the ordinary. When we get inside the building we walk down several flights of stairs that lead to the underground palace. There are heavy machines that surround us and about any type of weapon you could think of. Not only are there weapons but there's aircrafts. Toxic fumes can be smelt throughout the concrete bunker. There are hundreds of people, all working on something different. I begin to feel like I'm in a dream and none of this is real.

"This, Dominic is the mystery, few know," Hawkins says.

I walk around in pure fascination with everything around me. Many people approach Hawkins to shake his hand. Hawkins pulls me over to introduce me to the elite generals that run Sido. A bald guy named General Griffin shakes my hand.

"Your dad was a great fella, let me tell you something. Listen to everything that he had written up because it could go a long way into the destination of this world."

I genuinely take his advice to heart and continue to walk around looking at everything in amazement. After an hour of discovering the truth I decide I have made my decision about the documents.

"I'm ready to go home," I tell Hawkins.

He leads the way out of Sido and I take one last look at everything I've discovered. After leaving Sido we go to Rocky's Corner for pizza. When we get seated there I take a deep breath as I feel nothing but exhausted.

"What did you think?" My mom asks.

"It was fascinating."

"Now you know the truth to everything," Alyssa adds on.

"Yeah, I don't feel much satisfaction."

"I knew you wouldn't be satisfied but there's nothing more except for your decision," Hawkins says.

"Yeah I know, I'll keep you guessing on that since you guys did it to me."

"Fair enough."

We eat in peace enjoying the food and quality time together. I look around me seeing all the innocent lives that could have been lost. I question myself as a person if I don't reveal to the whole world about what's really happening. At the same time is it the right choice? I eat constantly questioning myself like never before. After I get done eating the world begins to spin again and I dart towards a bathroom. I puke my guts out this time and find myself laid out on the bathroom floor. I wipe my mouth up and head back to the table. When I get to the table no one is there, rather they're waiting for me outside. I walk outside as the moist, cool air hits my face making me feel a little better.

"Are you going to be okay?" Alyssa asks.

"Yes, just feeling anxious."

My mom hands me another pill for the nausea. The car ride home makes me sick to my stomach. Once we get home, I rush into my room and lay on my bed for the rest of the night, thinking about the decision that I must make and if it will be the right one. Alyssa comes in and lays next to me as she runs her fingers through my hair, which calms me down. No words are spoken as I'm exhausted from the day and her and I fall asleep.

For the first time in many days, there is sunshine. I wake up feeling much better than I did last night. Alyssa and I spend the morning watching movies and just try to be normal seventeen-year old's. For the first time in a while, I stop thinking about what is really going on and focus on what is happening in this moment. By the time lunch rolls around, my stomach is grumbling for food. I go to the kitchen and slap together sandwiches for Alyssa and I. When her and I finish eating we go for a walk down by the river. We skip rocks laughing and enjoying the moment.

Suddenly, while at the river the anxiety tries to hit me again, but I fight it away and take deep breaths. I try to keep my mind occupied instead of constantly thinking of random things that could trigger the panic attacks. I plan on revealing my decision after dinner and I pray that it's the right one. Alyssa and I walk back home hand in hand in silence. When we walk through the door my mom says, "Hey you two, dinner is done." Alyssa and I walk into the kitchen to find an unfamiliar woman sitting at the table.

I turn around to my mom. "Who is she?" I ask.

"A guest," my mom responds.

Alyssa and I sit next to her wondering who she is. Moments later my mom hands us each a plate of spaghetti. I eat it, not really feeling well but the woman chows down her plate. After I finish I throw my plate into the sink but before I could head off to my room my mom stops me.

"That women, that's Sidney Dobell. Go talk to her."

In somewhat of a shock I approach Sidney.

"Do you want to talk?" I ask Sidney.

She nods as her and I head downstairs. I sit next to her on an old couch that sits in a corner.

"I'm sorry, Dominic."

"Why?"

"I was sent here to save you."

"Sidney, the government is lying to you."

"Dominic it's not the government. Do you not remember why you're here?"

"What are you talking about?"

"I assure you that you know what I'm talking about."

"Uh, you're starting to freak me out."

"You're here to save the world."

"Yeah I kind of figured that out?"

"No, you haven't figured anything out."

"What's wrong with you?"

"Nothing?"

"Look, you seem sweet but I'm not feeling good," I say walking back upstairs.

I hear her tell me not to go but I can't deal with anymore craziness. When I get to the top of the stairs she tells me goodbye

168

crying. I shake my head and go lay down in my room. My mom comes in asking me about our conversation.

"Mom, she's crazy."

"She did seem odd, that's first time I ever seen her. Hawkins assured me she could help you with your decision."

"I didn't think anyone knew where she was?"

"Hawkins knows everything," my mom laughs.

I get up and head to the kitchen with my mind made up for what is to come. Everyone sits around the table as I express what I want to happen.

"I hope you guys won't be mad, but I decide to store these documentations away and forget about what never happened."

"Have mercy on us all," Hawkins jokes.

I store the safe in my closet with clothes thrown on top of it. With this decision, I now feel complete. The world will go on not knowing the truth because sometimes the truth is not always for the best.

# CHAPTER THIRTEEN

Months have gone by with no repercussion of my decision. Since then, life has been nothing but good. I showed Alyssa the ring, promising to be by her side for eternity and one day she'll be my bride. Hawkins resigned as the principal at Hot Springs High School and occasionally comes by to check on me. My mom continues to support me as I am to begin my senior year of high school. Sido was shut down leaving the public wondering what truly went on there. Only few know the truth and I'm determined to keep it that way.

I wake up with Alyssa by my side with today being our first day of our senior year. Luckily, Hawkins went back and dismissed my hour detention that I received on the last day of school. The summer is one I'll never forget for years to come, but I'm glad it's over with. I get ready, looking good for my last first day of high school. Part of me is excited to graduate but the other part of me isn't ready for that next step because of the unknown to come. My mom lends me her keys to take the truck to school. When I arrive at the school, everything is normal, just like it was last year. No one knew what was really happening except that I ended up in the hospital. For the first time in months, Alyssa and I will break apart since her and I have different classes throughout the day. In most of my classes, the teacher went over the syllabus making sure the class knows the rules and expectations for the year. I find myself with my eyes shut on numerous occasions due to the lack of sleep I got.

Once lunch rolls around, Alyssa and I are reunited and sit by ourselves, hating the school lunch. I finish the day off strong and what felt like days later the final bell rung. Alyssa and I depart back home where her and I spend the evening talking about our hopes and dreams for the future, while trying to put the past behind us.

The next several weeks continue just like the first day of school. Everything normal and no one talks to me unless it's school related. But a little after a month of school things begin to get strange.

I get up just like any typical day looking out the window to find black SUV's parked outside of my house. I throw on some clothes and walk near the vehicles but when they see me they take off. I go back inside to eat breakfast wondering what they wanted. Was it the government making sure I don't come out about the documents? Surely it's not, I think preparing to get ready for school. Alyssa comes out in her pajamas wrapping her arms around me while I brush my teeth.

"Babe, there were black SUV's outside the house this morning," I say.

"Tell your mom."

I go into the kitchen where my mom is making herself breakfast. At first, I stand there hesitant to ask but do anyway.

"Mom, do you know why there was black SUV's outside the house this morning?"

"Hmm no, it's probably nothing."

"The government isn't after me, are they?"

"Dominic," she says looking at me. "They won't mess with you knowing you have those documents."

"What's so authentic about them? It's just my dad's writing."

"Yeah, but I also contain the evidence."

"So, you don't think I'm in harm's way?"

"Not at all, just get through your last year of school."

I throw my lunch into my book bag and Alyssa and I head to school. When I arrive in the school parking lot I instantly spot the SUV's to my right. I get out of the truck slamming the door and lightly jogging towards the vehicles. While getting closer, the vehicles remain still. I get to one of the vehicles, but no one is inside. It suddenly hits me that whoever drives the SUV's are in the school. When I walk in the front doors I'm greeted by our new Principal, Dr. Miller. He tells me to follow him to his office, so I do.

I send a text to Hawkins joking about going to his old office. But when I get in the office I notice this isn't a joke.

"These men have a few questions for you," Dr. Miller tells me.

I shake their hands while they greet me and inform me that they're government agents.

"Dr. Miller would you mind stepping out of the office for a second?"

Dr. Miller steps out of the office for what feels like several minutes.

"Dominic, is that right?" A young agent asks.

"That's correct."

"Hi Dominic, my name is Agent Dukes. We know who you are and let me tell you something we aren't scared of what you have. Whatever you know will still happen one way or another whether you keep it to yourself or tell the whole world. But let me ask you, why didn't you tell the whole world?"

"I didn't feel like it was in the best interest for my country."

"See that's where you're wrong. You need to tell the world because it is in the best interest for this country. You happen to know the truth, having the power to help a world in need."

"Sir, why would you want me to release these documents?"

"Look Dominic, I was totally pro-government until I found out what was really going on. I stepped away and I'm currently being hunted down by other agents. You can save this world from a disaster that'll end humanity, or you can let the world crumble along with yourself."

"So, you're saying that they still plan to poison the citizens?"

"Exactly, but you're the only one that can speak out on it, since you have the evidence."

"What's in it for me?"

"Your life."

"So, no protection or anything?"

"Dominic, right now it's every man and woman for themselves."

"Bullshit, I can't believe anything you say."

"We promise that this is nothing but real."

"Let me tell you something Agent Dukes. I have been promised a lot of things in my past and ninety percent of them were broken. So, if you think I'm going to believe you of all people, you're in an idealistic world," I say walking out of the room.

I head to my first class late without a pass. The teacher tells me that I must go back and get a pass from the office, so I do. The agents are about to leave when I arrive at the office. Agents Dukes looks at me and makes his way towards me.

"Dominic, come outside with me really quick."

I get permission from the office, but I was hoping they would say no. Him and I walk outside and he just stands there for a couple of seconds.

"Look, do what you want, but I was sent here for your benefit and everyone else's. There's a lot that you don't understand but I want to tell you this. I work for a woman you may know by the name of Sidney Dobell. I know she's already tried warning you, but I want to talk in depth if you'll meet me for dinner tonight at Logan's Steakhouse around six."

"Just because I want to hear what you have to say, I will. But just know I'll have people around just in case you try something idiotic."

"I know, but just know we're on the same side."

I walk back into the school to continue the day. At lunch I explain everything to Alyssa that just happened. She is just as much worried as I am, but we decide to give Agent Dukes an opportunity to say what he has to say. Much of the day drug by but when three o'clock came I was out of there. I look at my phone seeing Hawkins messaged me back from earlier saying, "What did you do now?"

I tell him to come over to my house as soon as possible. Hawkins arrives shortly after I get home, so I explain everything to him and my mom. Between us we mutually decide that my mom, Hawkins, and Alyssa would sit at a different table but close by. I change out of my school clothes into more comfortable clothes like a t-shirt and shorts. Once five-fifty hits we all head to Logan's Steakhouse. I walk in by myself when we get there so they don't know who's with me. When I spot Agent Dukes, I take a seat across from him. Soon after Hawkins, Alyssa, and my mom sit down at chairs and the tables diagonal from us.

"How did I know you'd bring Roger Hawkins with you?" Agent Dukes asks shaking his head.

"How do you know him?"

"Hawkins and I are friends. Actually, all of this was his idea."

"No stop, you're lying he wouldn't do that."

"But I'm not, like I've said you don't know the whole truth."

"Hold on, I'll be right back," I say walking over towards the table Hawkins is sitting at.

"Hawkins, I thought the decision was mine? I didn't think you'd send people here to change a decision that I made months ago."

"I know, but I didn't know how to tell you the truth. I felt like you wouldn't have believed me."

"What do you mean? I've done nothing but trust you," I yell.

"Dominic lower your voice," my mom chips in.

"No, I want to know the truth."

"Dominic, I didn't think you'd be able to handle the truth but now it's a must that you know but I refuse to tell you," Hawkins says.

"Fine, but after I find out the truth don't expect me to trust you again."

"Okay fair enough, now go talk to Agent Dukes."

I walk over to the booth to continue the conversation with Agent Dukes.

"So, what's the truth? I want to know," I exclaim.

"Fine. I've told you that you could prevent human existence. What I didn't tell you was you never existed the last time this ordeal occurred."

"I'm confused."

"Look around you, what you see won't exist tomorrow if you don't reveal the documents. Life on earth is being given a second chance but without you it's over."

"Sir, I'm pretty sure that's wrong."

"Do you not get it Dominic? You were sent here to prevent the world from ending again!"

"You're here to save the world, but had no problem destroying what Alyssa and I had." -Spencer

# Acknowledgments

I would like to Acknowledge the people on behalf of the success of this book.

First off, I want to thank my amazing parents for supporting all my decisions. You two have been there for me no matter what and for that I'm thankful.

My grandma, Shirley. You have been a big contributor to my success with this book. You read every chapter after I finished them to give me feedback. Without you, this book would not be alive because when I didn't believe in this story, you did.

My cover designer, Justin Cappon. A huge thank you for answering all my questions that I had and for making my amazing cover.

Lastly, I would like to thank everybody that has been a part of this amazing journey. No words can explain my appreciation to the ones that took time out of their schedules to better this story.

www.ingramcontent.com/pod-product-compliance
Lightning Source LLC
Chambersburg PA
CBHW060422130626
46555CB00005B/2169